CBSE

[Central Board of Secondary Education]

ENTREPRENEURSHIP

CLASS - XII

Content Table

Chapter No	Chapters	Page No
1.	Entrepreneurial Opportunity	2-13
2.	Entrepreneurial Planning	14-26
3.	Enterprise Marketing	27-41
4.	Enterprise Growth Strategies	42-54
5.	Business Arithmetic	55-63
6.	Resource Mobilization	64-70

Chapter- 1 Entrepreneurial Opportunity

Introduction

Entrepreneurial opportunity is the point at which identifiable consumer demand meets the feasibility of satisfying the requested product or service. In the field of entrepreneurship, specific criteria need to be met to move from an idea into an opportunity.

There are a lot of opportunities in the world of business, which everyone might not be able to spot. An entrepreneur should be able to spot it. Business opportunity can be described as an economic idea which can be implemented to create a business enterprise and earn profits. Before selecting an opportunity, the entrepreneur has to ensure two things-
- There is a good market for the product he is going to produce
- The rate of return on the investment is attractive to be accepted by him

Only when the entrepreneur is able to fulfil these two criteria, he/she can be successful. Quite often, a question arises - Can all ideas be converted into opportunities? Mostly entrepreneurs conceive an idea and start their business without even analysing the market which often leads to satisfying their own ego, and the result is that they launch a product that has very few customers.

Elements of a business opportunity
A business opportunity may be described as an attractive economic idea which could be implemented to create a business, earn profits and ensure further growth. A business opportunity has five elements which are as follows:
- Assured market scope
- An attractive and acceptable rate of return on investment
- Practicability of the idea
- Competence of the entrepreneur to encash it
- Potential of future growth

Meaning of Entrepreneurship, Entrepreneur, Enterprise:
Entrepreneurship (PROCESS): Entrepreneurship is the process of identifying opportunities in the marketplace and arranging for resources to explain the identified opportunity in order to harness long-term gains.
Entrepreneur (PERSON): An entrepreneur is a person who is a catalytic agent in converting a situation into an opportunity and setting up a business in the process.
In the words of Peter F Drucker Entrepreneur is one who always searches for an opportunity.
Enterprise (OUTCOME): The outcome of the Entrepreneurship process is called Enterprise. It provides goods and services, creates jobs, contributes to national income, export, and also contributes to the overall economic development.

Sensing Entrepreneurial Opportunities

Entrepreneurs perceive opportunities, synthesize the available information and analyse emerging patterns that escape the attention of other people. They are people with vision, capable of persuading others such as customers, partners, employees and suppliers to see the opportunity, share and support it.

Factors Involved in Sensing Opportunities
To sense an entrepreneurial opportunity, an entrepreneur employs his/her sharpened skills of observation, analysis and synthesis to identify an opening. The most important factors involved in the process are:
- Ability to perceive and preserve basic ideas which could be used commercially
- Ability to harness different sources of information
- Vision and creativity

Perceiving and sensing opportunities
Sensing entrepreneurial opportunities: Meaning: It is a process of perceiving the needs and problems of people and society and arriving at creative solutions. In this, an entrepreneur employs his\her sharpened skills of observation, analysis, and synthesis to identify an opening.

Factors involved in sensing opportunities:

To sense opportunity, an entrepreneur employs his skill, observation, vision, knowledge, and creativity. The most important factors involved in sensing an opportunity are:
- Ability to perceive and preserve basic ideas
- Ability to harness different sources of knowledge and information
- Vision and creativity

Ability to perceive and preserve basic ideas:

Spotting an idea often triggers the process of sensing an opportunity. The following are the various sources of emerging an idea: (ICICIP)

Problem: Most of the time solution of a problem becomes an opportunity. E.g. Businesses dealing in generators and inverters grow due to the problem of electricity. A problem gives rise to business opportunities.

Change: All the environmental changes, be it social, legal, or technological give rise to the new business opportunity. For e.g products like zero-calorie coke, multigrain bread is the result of the movement of society towards health consciousness.

Inventions: New products or services lead to new business opportunities. E.g. Pen drives, I -pods, digital cameras are business opportunities brought by inventions.

Competition: Whenever someone tries to beat the competition, he resorts to new and improved ideas. This is the only way to survive in the market.

Innovation: It means creating new things of value as well as processing the added value to existing products or services. E.g. Computers to tablets

Ability to harness different sources of information: There are various sources from which information can be gathered like magazines, books, journals, seminars trade shows, friends, family members, etc. The information gathered from various sources must be analyzed, verified, and utilized properly. Many people get the information but only some analyze the information, harness and try to get the best from it.

Vision and creativity: Many people can see the same problem but an entrepreneur is the one who finds its most creative solution with his vision and creativity. With his vision, he converts the solution into a business opportunity. Through their vision and creativity they constantly:

(a) Overcome adversity

(b) exercise control over the business

(c) Make a significant difference.

Environment Scanning

Business Environment can be defined as all those conditions and external forces to a business unit under which it operates. Business environment may be defined as all those conditions and forces external to a business unit under which it operates. Entrepreneurship does not emerge and grow spontaneously. Rather, it is dependent upon several economic, social, political, legal and other factors.

Careful monitoring of an organization's internal and external environment for detecting early signs of opportunities and threats that may influence its current and future plans.

Why do we need to scan our environment? In a rapidly changing environment, one rule of thumb applies: If you don't adapt, you don't endure. This is the core idea behind environmental scanning. Definitions of the term refers to the means by which organizations gather information on changing conditions and incorporate those observations into a process where necessary changes are made. The right information, combined with the right adaptations, can determine an organization's future viability. If an entrepreneur is not aware of the environment surrounding his/her business, he/she is sure to fail.

Importance of environment

Sensitivity to environmental factors is crucial for an entrepreneur. If a company is able to adapt to its environment, it would succeed in the long run. For example, Sony is failing to understand the changing trends in mobile phones and therefore losing it's market share.

Identification of Opportunities to get first mover advantage

The businessman who are able to understand and scan the opportunities of business environment at early stage get maximum benefit or can capture a big share in the market. They can go much ahead of their competitors. For example, Goodlass Nerolac was the first company to understand that soon there will be a great demand of car painting in India once Maruti will sign contract with Suzuki. So Nerolac prepared itself for that opportunity in advance by signing contract with Kansai Paints , which increased its production capacity to fulfil the demand of Maruti.

Formulation of strategies and policies
Strategies are the types of plan which are made to face the competitors. Environment scanning helps in early identification of threats from competitors for which counter strategies are formulated to face the competitors. Also opportunities can be capitalised by suitable strategic policies.

Tapping useful Resources
Businessman have to supply goods to market according to demand in the market. To supply output they need input, raw material etc. They acquire raw material and other resources keeping in mind the demand in the environment. Which helps in doing the best utilisation of resources because scanning of environment helps a businessman to know and understand the taste and demand of customers. E.g with the demand for flat screen T.V. manufacturers are collecting resources necessary to manufacture flat screen colour T.V. rather than collecting resources of Black and White T.V.

Better Performance
With continuous scanning of the business environment, companies can easily improve their performance. By making the changes in the internal environment and matching it to the external environment, Organisations can prosper and improve their market share. E.g. Weston company which could not cooperate with the changing environment started suffering loss and lost its name in the T.V. market whereas BPL and Onida did scan the environment well and are still running successfully in the market.

Sensitisation of entrepreneurs to cope up with rapid changes
A keen watch on trends in the environment would help sensitise the entrepreneurs to become proactive towards the needs of customers, changing trends, government policy, technology etc. e.g. Reliance trends keep on changing its clothes with changes in fashion to gain an edge over its competitors.

Image building
If a company is sensitive to the external environment, it will come out with new products and services by or building our better goods and services which help in image building and reputation. E.g nowadays transport companies are offering online bookings.

The benefits of understanding the relevant environment of business are:
Identification of opportunities to get first mover advantage
By keeping in touch with the changes in the external environment, an enterprise can identify opportunities and find strategies to capitalise on the opportunities at the earliest. For example, Volvo, the Swedish brand, has 74% share in the luxury bus segment as it had entered India earlier.

Formulation of strategies and policies
It helps in identifying threats and opportunities in the market. These can serve as the basis of formulation of strategies to counter threats and capitalise on opportunities in the market.

Tapping useful resources
If the company has a thorough knowledge of the external environment, it can tap raw materials, technology and even financial resources from the market at economical prices, at the right time.

Better performance
Proper understanding of the various elements of the external environment is necessary to take timely action to deal with threats and avail opportunities for the purpose of improvement in the performance of the firm.

Sensitization of entrepreneurs to cope up with rapid changes
A keen watch on the trends in the environment would help sensitise the entrepreneur to changing technology, competition, government policies and changing needs of the customers. For example, trends in clothing.

Image building
If a company is sensitive to the external environment, it will come out with new products and services to meet the requirements of the customers. This would build the image or reputation of the firm in the eyes of the general public. For example, call-radio taxis with additional features like GPS systems, online booking etc.

SWOT Analysis Framework

Analysis of environment
Environment analysis is the process of monitoring the economic and non-economic environment, to determine the opportunities and threats to an organisation. Such an analysis involves data collection, information processing and forecasting to provide a rational basis for developing goals and strategies for business survival and growth. Information for environmental scanning can be collected from several sources. These include.

- verbal information from customers, wholesalers, retailers, distributors, consultants, etc.
- records of companies
- government publications
- publications by various financial institutions
- formal studies conducted by strategic planners

Meaning: It is the process of monitoring the economic and noneconomic environment to determine the opportunities and threats to an organization.

This process of environment analysis involves:
- Data Collection
- Information processing
- Forecasting to provide developing goals and strategies for business survival and growth.

Sources of Information for environment scanning / Sources of data Collection for environment scanning:
- Verbal information from customers, wholesalers, retailers, distributors, consultants etc.
- Records of companies
- Government publications
- Publications by financial institutions
- Formal studies conducted by strategic planners.

The data obtained is processed and analyzed with the help of quantitative and qualitative techniques.

The flowchart shows that the opportunity perceived by the entrepreneur has to be tested for its economic viability against important environmental parameters to arrive at a sound business choice.

Types of Environment Analysis/ business environment
There are two types of environment analysis done which help in identifying the SWOT (Strength, Weaknesses, Opportunities, Threats)

Internal Analysis/ Internal environment: It is specific to company's internal strengths and weaknesses. It involves those factors which remain under the control of the entrepreneur. E.g. land, production , capital ,top management structure, companies financial resources, its image and brand equity. These factors help in identifying its strengths and weaknesses.

External Analysis/ External environment: These are those factors which put pressure on the firm from outside. These help to identify opportunities and threats present in the environment.

Environmental Factors
Entrepreneurship environment refers to the various forces within which various small, medium and large enterprises operate. These factors exert influence upon each other and do not operate in isolation. Business environment consists of two levels, i.e., micro environment and macro environment.

Entrepreneurship environment refers to the various forces within which various small, medium and large enterprises operate. These factors affect each other.

Business Environment consists of two levels.
- Microenvironment
- Macroenvironment

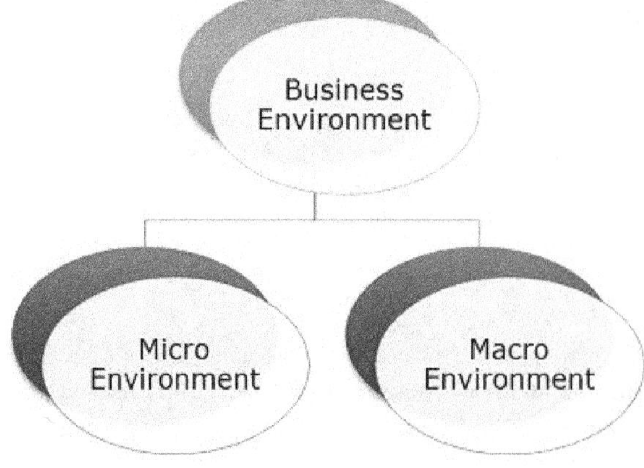

Every business organization is a part of the business environment, within which it operates. No entity can function in isolation because there are many factors that closely or distantly surrounds the business, which is known as a business environment. It is broadly classified into two categories, i.e. microenvironment, and macro environment. The former affects the working of a particular business only, to which they relate to, while the latter affects the functioning of all the business entities, operating in the economy.

Microenvironment

Microenvironment refers to the environment which is in direct contact with the business organization and can affect the routine activities of business straight away. It is associated with a small area in which the firm functions.

The microenvironment is a collection of all the forces that are close to the firm. These forces are very particular for the said business only. They can influence the performance and day to day operations of the company, but for the short term only. Its elements include suppliers, competitors, marketing intermediaries, customers and the firm itself.

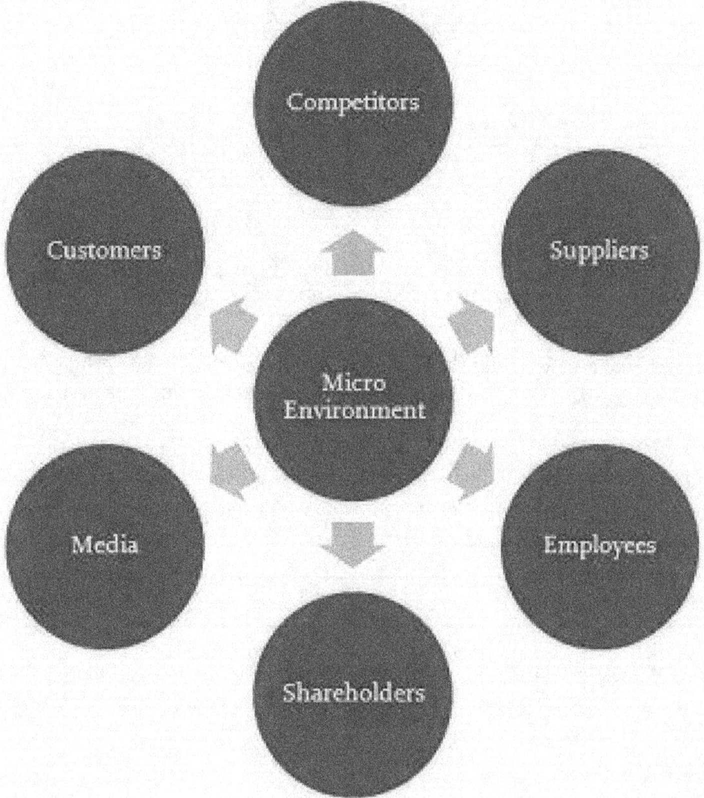

- Suppliers are the ones who provide inputs to the business like raw material, equipment and so on.
- Competitors are the rivals, which compete with the firm in the market and resources as well.
- Marketing intermediaries may include wholesalers, distributors, and retailers that make a link between the firm and the customers.
- Customers / Consumers are the ones who purchase the goods for their own consumption. They are considered as the king of business.
- The firm itself is an aggregate of a number of elements like owners like shareholders or investors, employees and the board of directors.

Macro Environment

The general environment within the economy that influences the working, performance, decision making and strategy of all business groups at the same time is known as Macro Environment. It is dynamic in nature. Therefore it keeps on changing.

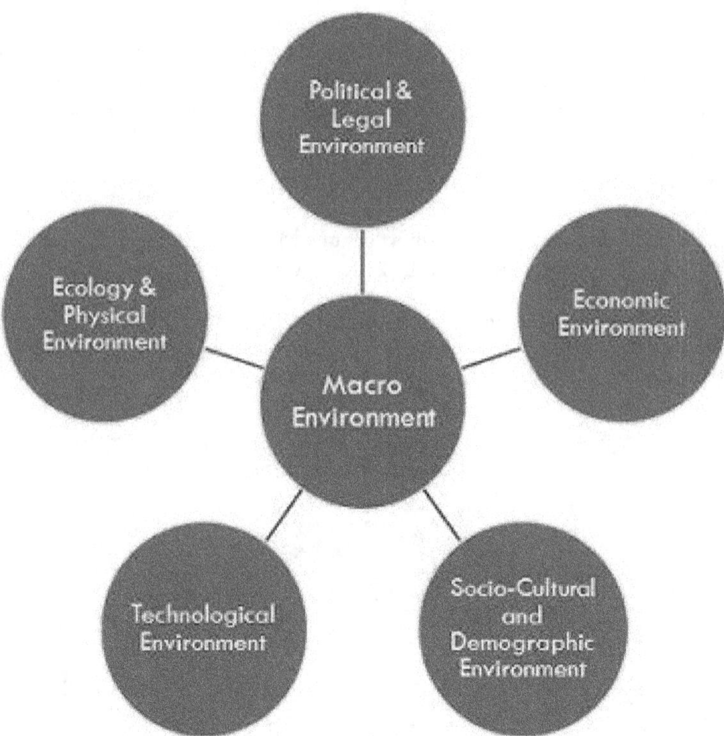

It constitutes those outside forces that are not under the control of the firm but have a powerful impact on the firm's functioning. It consists of individuals, groups, organizations, agencies and others with which the firm deals during the course of its business.

The study of Macro Environment is known as PESTLE Analysis. PESTLE stands for the variables that exist in the environment, i.e. Political, Economic, Socio-cultural, Technological, Legal and Environmental. These variables, consider both economic and non-economic factors like social concerns, government policies, family structure, population size, inflation, GDP aspects, income distribution, ethnic mix, political stability, taxes, and duties, etc.

Problem Identification

Meaning: When there is a roadblock in a situation, which poses a conflict and forces you to find a solution then this roadblock is a problem and when one identifies this roadblock, it is called problem identification.

Objectives of problem identification:
- It should clearly state the problem.
- It should identify the target group facing the problem.
- It should find the market acceptability of the solution to the problem.

Uses of Problem Identification:
Problem Identification helps the entrepreneur in the following ways:
- To understand the needs and problems of the market.
- To bring out new product in the market.
- To become creative.
- To increase employment generation.
- To increase national income of the country.

Idea Generation
Meaning: Idea generation is a process of creating developing and communicating ideas that are abstract, concrete, or virtual. It includes the process of developing the idea through creativity and innovation and bringing the concept to reality.

Idea fields

Meaning: Idea fields can be defined as ' Convenient frames of reference for streamlining the process of generation of ideas. Idea fields help in enlarging the scope of thinking and also give the entrepreneur the benefit of structuring ideas based on convenient frames of reference.

Sources of idea fields: (NESTCM)

Natural Resources: Ideas can be generated based on natural resources. A product or service may be desired from forest resources, agriculture, horticulture, minerals, marine or aqua minerals, animal husbandry, wind, sun, and human resources. E.g. If we think of getting ideas in the field of forest resources, we can think of forest produce, wood based products etc.

Existing products or services: Another field to generate new ideas can be improving the existing products and services. We can use the latest technology in existing products or make them cheaper by producing them with cost saving method etc. thinking about innovative ways of packaging etc. A great business idea combines skill with imagination and market demand. Entrepreneur who look at the ways to make an existing product or service better can be as successful as those who create and invent products. E.g In case of Britannia Breads the company is constantly improving on its existing product and bringing out new variants like Atta bread, multigrain bread, garlic bread.

While it may seem like only good can come from improving, adding to, or changing different products around, This is not always the case, It must be done skillfully or else other problems can arise. It can benefit the business in the following manner:

Keep up with the competition: If the products or services are of constantly changing nature, you have to stay aware of the changes and adopt such changes. This will help an entrepreneur to stay ahead than his competitor.e.g In case of a mobile manufacturing unit, the manufacturer has to constantly upgrade his process with the change in technology.

Increase Sales: Upgradation and Improvement in existing product line can help an entrepreneur to increase his sales, which can further lead to increase in profits. So the change should be such that it should help in increasing the revenue of the business. E.g Publishing house engaged in the publication of competitive books ventures into school books. The addition in product line will definitely increase the revenues of the firm.

Market or demand driven ideas: One of the important methods of generating idea is Market research. While assessing the market, an entrepreneur has to prepare details about demand (taste of consumer, fashion), trends od supply (Quantity supplied by already existing suppliers), and customer preference. Market research is an organised effort to gather information about target markets or customers. It includes social and opinion research and is the systematic gathering and interpretation of information about individuals or organisations using statistical and analytical methods and techniques of applied social science to support decision making.

Difference between Market research and Marketing Research

Marketing Research is concerned specifically with marketing processes.

Basis for comparison	Market research	Marketing research
Meaning	A study undertaken to collect information about the market statistics, is known as market research.	Marketing research is the systematic and objective study, analysis and interpretation of problem related to marketing activities.
Branch of	Marketing Research	Marketing Information System
Scope	Limited	Wide
Nature	Specific	Generic
Involves	Research of marketplace and the buyer's behavior within that market.	Research of all the aspects of marketing.
Dependency	Dependent	Independent
Purpose	To check the viability of the product in the target market.	To make effective decisions regarding marketing activities and to keep control on the marketing of economic output.

Market Research is concerned with Markets:

Trading related ideas: Trading means buying of goods and services and selling them to consumers at profit. Advantage of trading are that is less risky and easy to launch.Today the scope of trade has enlarged to local trade, import trade, export, e commerce , Umbrella markets, departmental stores, chain storesetc. The trader must be aware of the trend in the market. The trader must study in detail the needs and wants of customers to win over the competitors. To survive in the market new entrants will have to acquire skills, competencies and knowledge required to launch , manage and expand business opportunities.

Service sector Related Ideas: Service sector refers to providing services either by entrepreneur himself or by hiring some employees. Entrepreneur must own the enterprise and provide service through his enterprise. The reason for service sector being the most growing field now a days is emerging knowledge societies and advancement in information and technology.

Some of the interesting opportunities in service sector are as follows:
Creative Efforts: Creativity is an important idea field. It is not only used to spot and harness opportunities. It can also be applied to develop new products and services. Two businessmen can have same qualification, same capital and same products but the entrepreneur with creativity and skill will always have an edge over the other businessman. Generally creativity comes as a result of problem solving. Whenever people face problem, to overcome those problems new products and services are created.

Spotting Trends

Meaning: Trend spotting refers to the Identification/recognition of the latest market trends. It helps the entrepreneur to bring changes in their products or services in accordance with the trends prevailing in the market. The success of the enterprise depends on the effectiveness of the trend spotting.

Entrepreneurs identify the trends themselves or with the help of the trend-spotter. In general trend, spotting takes place through one of the following activities. It includes Read trends, Talk trends, Watch trends and Think trend.

Read trends: Entrepreneurs spot the trends by reading through various sources like

- Online resources like websites, influential bloggers, e-mail newsletters, websites etc
- newspapers, magazines and other publications like industry publications.
- thought leaders who are experts in a particular industry or sector

Usually, these trends originate from international cities like London, Paris, and Tokyo. So entrepreneurs keep an eye on the changes in the trend taking place in these places. Not all trends will be useful. Entrepreneurs use their discretion to make a quick decision regarding accepting or discarding these trends.

Talk trends: Entrepreneurs discuss about the trends with:

- **Entrepreneurs who have similar interests:** In-person discussions usually take place at their industry specific trade association events or conferences etc. In addition to this they also participate in social networking sites, forums, discussion groups, smart phone apps etc. Usually, they take advantage of the existing networks. It is also possible that they start their own online discussion platforms.
- **Discuss with the customers:** They discuss with the customers both online and offline. Customer inputs are procured through social networking sites, surveys, forums, discussion groups. The trends are also spotted by observing consumer opinions in the ratings and reviews sites.

Watch trends: The trend among the consumers can be perceived by visiting the frequent hang out locations of their consumer group like.

- a shopping mall
- eateries
- trade shows
- cinemas
- college campuses
- marriages

The entrepreneurs spend time watching what their consumer group is eating or drinking or wearing or showing interest in.

Think trend: All the information gathered through reading, discussion and careful observations is analyzed. This help the entrepreneur to build trend-spotter-brain. The analysis will open up connections between different observations which will help in coming up with a potential entrepreneurial opportunity by improving an existing product or service or coming up with a new one altogether.

Creativity and Innovation

Creativity
Creativity is the first stage in the process of innovation, providing the stimulus for opportunity discovery and new venture creation.

The creative process:
Creativity is important to entrepreneurs. The process of creativity involves the following steps: (IPIIVI)

Idea germination: It is the stage where an entrepreneur recognizes that an opportunity exists. The creative idea emerges from the deep interest or curiosity of the entrepreneur. He then explores and exploits it to its best potential. The idea can also germinate from the need of finding a solution to some problem. If the perceived problem is motivated enough to capture the individual's interest then it leads to stage II.

- **Preparation:** The idea germinated in the above step is evaluated and a solution is identified. If the solution leads to an innovative product or service, a market research is performed to identify the opportunities to exploit the idea. Once it is concluded that the idea has potential growth opportunity, the entrepreneur will proceed to next stage
- **Incubation:** In this phase, all required information is gathered from various sources. The information is analyzed to evaluate the various pros and cons of implementing the idea. If Entrepreneur feels here positives of the idea are more than negatives, then he moves for next stage
- **Illumination:** In this phase, a detailed plan to implement the idea is laid out. The entrepreneur will start accumulating the capital, procuring the raw material, laying out the process, deciding the policy etc starts out.
- **Verification:** In this stage, the idea is turned into reality and the entrepreneur will start monitoring the outcome. The entrepreneur will start seeing obstacles and take necessary steps to overcome the obstacles, to move the enterprise towards its goal.

Innovation

Meaning: Innovation can be defined as a process followed by an entrepreneur to transform an idea into a commercially viable product or service.

Following are the Elements/ Steps in the innovation process: (AOIC)

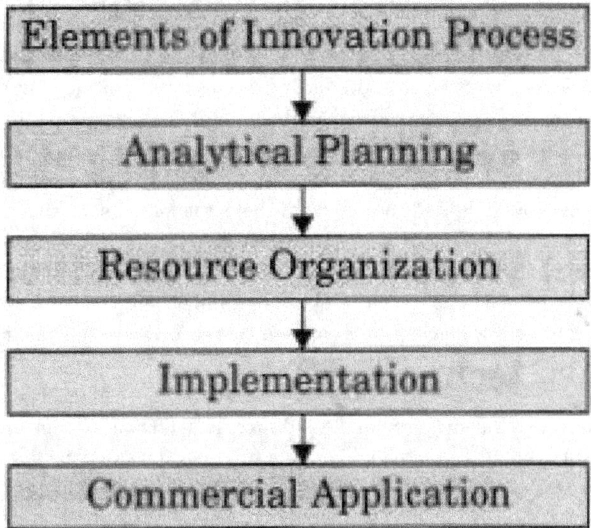

Analytical Planning: Do a thorough analysis and
- Identify the features of the product or service
- identify the design
- identify all the resources required to implement

Resource Organization:

Arrange all the required resources like
- money
- machine
- Manpower
- Material
- Technology

Implementation: Use the organized resources to implement the plan and start manufacturing a product or providing a service.

Commercial application:
- Supply the product or service to the customer.
- Make profits

- Recognize and reward the employees
- Share profits with the investors and other stake holders.

Selecting the Right Opportunity

The entrepreneur should look into various factors before deciding on the opportunity. Even if the opportunity looks promising, an entrepreneur should look into the environmental factors before choosing the best opportunity.

If you have decided to be an entrepreneur and you don't want to start from bottom level, buying into a home-based or other business opportunities, distributorship, franchise, or licensee opportunity are the great options. Still, finding the best one that is right for you can be a big challenge. Here some factors to choose from. So how do you improve in on the ones that warrant further analysis and consideration on your part?

Here are some tips for narrowing the field and selecting wisely:
Look for a track record: The span of time that a company has been in business tells you a lot in selecting the right business opportunities. There will be history of success or even failure that you can learn from. Brand recognition and reputation that goes along with it is priceless. The longer a company exists, the more likely you can verify profitability and whole success within its ranks, giving you a better understanding of the calculated risk, you would be taking. This is not at all to say that a new company is not worth to start, but you better be sure to do your due diligence up a serious way before you buy what they're selling.

Verify viability: There are lot of advertisement like "get rich quick." If someone tells you that you can also become very wealthy overnight by putting only very little effort, just be careful. There is no easy way to make money. If it was that simple, we all will be millionaires. Make sure by choosing the correct business opportunities.

Mind your marketability: You might be giving the good product or service out there and have no demand for it simply because you don't do homework for your business opportunities. You have to know about your competition in your marketplace. You have to know about the demand for your products or services. Who wants and needs they? You should know how what you are offering is different, whether it's regard with quality, features, and cost. If you're selling is truly unique, then great that's your niche. If not, and very little, then you need to know how saturated your market is before you start something.

Look for a profitability timeline: The thumb rule when opening a new business from business opportunities is that it can take six months to a year for profits to come in. It is not only to be prepared financially, you need to look for business opportunities that are known to you or you feel confident will give profits soon. Of course, if you're starting in part-time, it is really the smart way to go at first.

Seek out training and ongoing support: The most reputable and successful business opportunities offer comprehensive training and ongoing support to their stake holders. You're looking for a trust worthy company that is known for its integrity. All of that starts at the top. Do your homework on benchmarking any company which you are thinking of affiliating yourself with.

Avoid the newest fad or craze: Except you know you're looking for business opportunities with a very short shelf life you want to stay away from companies that jump on board with the newest trend, especially if it seems passing.

Beware of your where and how: Where you run your business and how have great consequences in your wallet and your overall success. Does the business you are interested require a storefront? Could you do business online? Will you work from home? Is the business model you are exploring an ideal home based type? Is the business requires you to store inventory? Buy a business vehicle? Operate and store heavy machinery or materials? If so, you should consider everything from creating additional storage space to the distribution.

Have your eyes open when it comes to what it takes: Doing a business is easy...on paper. Having it profitable requires hard work. Do not kid yourself. Entrepreneurship is not for the risk averse. If it is your personality, find a job working for someone else.

Calculate your risk carefully and minimize it the best you can: Few business opportunities require very little money up front to get begin, meaning the comparative risk should you fail is significantly low. Other opportunities can be costly on the front end. It's significant that you clearly know why you want to start your own business in the first place. Do you want to make money for your current income? Or do you want to create a long term business in an industry that offers career path? How much do you want to or can you invest at start up? What are you risking in return exactly? Do you have a comprehensive business plan? If you don't, you need because, when you fail to plan, you plan to fail and that's just risky too.

Multiple Choice Questions

1. The relationship between opportunity and entrepreneur is:

    A. Water and Fish   **B.** Animal and Forest

    C. Lion and Goat   **D.** None of these

Answer: A

Explanation:

The relationship between opportunity and entrepreneur is Water and Fish.

2. It is __________ to give due consideration to internal re- sources before initiating a particular decision.

    A. Necessary   **B.** Unnecessary

    C. Lossable   **D.** Profitable

Answer: A

Explanation:

It is Necessary to give due consideration on internal re- sources before initiating a particular decision.

3. The products which are in more demand:

    A. More Profitable   **B.** More Lossable

    C. Equal   **D.** None of the above

Answer: A

Explanation:

The products which are in more demand are More Profitable.

4. Business opportunity relates with _______.

    A. Commercially feasible projects   **B.** Personal feasible projects

    C. (A) and (B) both   **D.** None of the above

Answer: A

Explanation:

Business opportunity relates to Commercially feasible projects.

5. Which of the following factors affecting identification of business opportunities?

    A. Volume of internal demand   **B.** Created opportunity

    C. Existing opportunities in the environment   **D.** None of these

Answer: A

Explanation:

Volume of internal demand is factors affecting identification of business opportunities.

6. Which of the following is a kind of opportunity?

    A. First opportunity   **B.** Created opportunity

    C. Last opportunity   **D.** None of the above

Answer: B

Explanation:

Created opportunity is a kind of opportunity.

7. Which of the following is a element of sensing op- portunities?

    A. Ability to perceive   **B.** Insight into the change

    C. Innovative quality   **D.** All of these

Answer: D

Explanation:

Ability to perceive, Insight into the change, Innovative quality is a element of sensing the op- portunities.

8. Entrepreneur is:

    A. Manager   **B.** Director

    C. Employee   **D.** Risk taker

Answer: D

Explanation:

Entrepreneur is Risk taker.

9. Which of the following is a problem connected with Business ?

    A. Profit   **B.** Money

    C. Sale   **D.** Risk management

Answer: D

Explanation:

Risk management is a problem connected with Business.

10. A positive personality trait of a creative person can be:

    A. Artistic   **B.** Open-minded

    C. Sense of Humor   **D.** All of the above

Answer: D

Explanation:

A positive personality trait of a creative person can be Artistic, Open-minded and Sense of Humor.

Chapter - 2 Entrepreneurial Planning

Introduction

If one is planning to start a business or is interested in expanding an existing one, an important decision relates to the choice of the form of organisation. The most appropriate form is determined by weighing the advantages and disadvantages of each type of organisation against one's own requirements.

A business organisation is an establishment intended to carry commercial business by producing goods or services and meet the customers' needs. Most of the organisations have a standard such as social structure, purpose goals, utilisation of resources, rules and regulations, etc.

The state law regulates the establishment of the business, and IRS law controls the tax incurred for business. So, how much tax business should pay depends on what form of business one owns.

Forms of business organisation

- An enterprise is a separate and distinct unit, institutionally arranged to conduct any type of business activity. It needs to combine the necessary things such as materials, tools, equipment, working space and bring together all of them in a systematic and effective manner to accomplish the entrepreneur's desired objective.
- Thus, every business entity needs to select an appropriate legal structure or framework to work in. This legal structure determines the extent of ownership and responsibility of proprietor(s). Appropriate form of organisation strongly influences the enterprise's success and future prospects.
- Once selected, changing the 'form' is quite a complex, time consuming and costly affair.
- Thus, every business entity needs to select an appropriate legal structure or framework to work in. This legal structure determines the extent of ownership and responsibility of proprietor(s). Appropriate form of organisation strongly influences the enterprise's success and future prospects.
- From the point of view **of ownership and management**, business enterprises may be broadly classified under three categories. **1) Private sector enterprises 2) Public sector enterprises 3) Joint sector enterprises**

Public Sector Enterprise

When business enterprises are owned, controlled and operated by public authorities, with welfare as primary and profit as secondary goals, they are called as public sector enterprises. Either the whole or most of the investment in these undertakings is done by the Government(s). These enterprises have the following forms of organisation:

- Departmental undertaking
- Public corporations
- Government companies

Factors to be considered while selecting form of organisation

- Vision regarding the size and nature of the business.
- The level of control the entrepreneur wishes to have.
- The level of "structure" entrepreneur is willing to deal with.
- The business vulnerability to lawsuits.
- Tax implications of the different organizational structures.
- Expected profit (or loss) of the business

Private Enterprise

The private sector or enterprise are the businesses that are owned by a private group or an individual. Different types of businesses under private enterprises are a partnership, sole proprietorship, cooperative, and company.

The private sector is the segment of a national economy that is owned, controlled, and managed by private individuals or enterprises. The private sector has a goal of making money and employs more workers than the public sector. A private sector organization is created by forming a new enterprise or privatizing a public sector organization. A large private sector corporation may be privately or publicly traded. Businesses in the private sector drive down prices for goods and services while competing for consumers' money; in theory, customers do not want to pay more for something when they can buy the same item elsewhere at a lower cost.

Types of Private Sector Businesses

The private sector is a very diverse sector and makes up a big part of many economies. It is based on many different individuals, partnerships, and groups. The entities that form the private sector include:

- Sole proprietorships
- Partnerships
- Small and mid-sized businesses
- Large corporations and multinationals
- Professional and trade associations
- Trade unions

Joint sector enterprises

The joint sector represents a new ideology of economic management geared to sub serve a new economic system.

The term is applied to an under-taking only when both its ownership and control are effectively shared between public sector agen-cies on the one hand and a private group on the other.

According to JRD Tata a joint sector enterprise is intended to form a partnership between the pri-vate sector and the Govt. in which the govt. par-ticipation of the capital will not be less than 26 p.c., the routine management will be normally in the hands of the private sector partner and control and supervision will be duly exercised by a governing board on which Government is adequately repre-sented.

Features of Joint Sector:

Joint sector enterprises may be brought into being by any of the following ways:

(i) The Central Govt. and private entrepre-neurs may jointly set up new enterprises. Sometimes the Central Govt. and one or more State Govts, together may set up enterprises in partnership with the pri-vate sector.

(ii) The State Govt. or their industrial devel-opment corporations may set up new companies jointly with private partners, involving equity participation by both the partners.

(iii) Public financial institutions may, through equity participation or conver-sion of loans or debentures into equity, transform enterprises promoted by pri-vate entrepreneurs into joint sector com-panies.

(iv) The existing private enterprises may be transformed into joint sector enterprises by the govt. or govt. companies acquir-ing a part of the equity or converting debt into equity or by contributing to an increase in the share capital.

(v) The existing public sector companies may be transformed into joint sector en-terprises through the sale of some eq-uity shares to private entrepreneurs or the general public.

Suitability of sole proprietorship form of business

The success or failure of an enterprise depends upon the intelligence, competence, and sensible decision-making capacity of the entrepreneur. Before opting for a sole proprietorship, an entrepreneur should carefully compare and evaluate the pros and cons of this form. Basically, this type of form is suitable when:

- Capital requirement is limited
- Confidentiality/secrecy is important
- Market is local
- Goods are of artistic nature or demands a customized approach
- Quick decision–making is necessary
- Size of the venture is small.

Legal formalities involved: A sole proprietorship does not need to be registered therefore an inexpensive manner of commencing business. However, in order to start a sole proprietorship, an entrepreneur requires certain industry-specific licenses. A few general factors are:

- **Business name**: free to select a trading name
- **Service tax registration**: Form ST 1 is to be filled for registration if the taxable services are more than 10 lakh for a financial year.
- **VAT/CST registration**: If proprietorship is selling tangible goods within a state then VAT applies,
- if it is inter-state then CST applies (its imperative). (CST – Central sales tax) (VAT- value-added tax.
- Others: PAN Card no. of the sole proprietor, bank account no. in the name of sole proprietorship business, Shops & Establishment License, Employee Provident Fund Registration, or Importer Exporter Code (if in export-import business) as and where applicable, have to be complied with.

- **Payment of taxes**: A sole trader has to ensure his/her business meets the state and federal taxation requirements. Due to the fact that legally, a sole tradership and a sole trader are a single entity, the sole trader bears the taxes of the business.

Partnership (two heads being better than one)

Limitations of Sole Proprietorship

Partnership form of organization has developed due to the inherent limitations of sole proprietorship i.e.
a) Limited capital
b) Limited managerial ability
c) Limited continuity

Partnership

Meaning:A partnership is an association of two or more persons to carry on, as co-owners, a business and to share its profits and losses. Thus, two or more persons may form a partnership by making a written or oral agreement called a partnership deed to carry a business jointly and share its proceeds.

Characteristics of partnership: (U – CRAME- IT- Please)

Two or more persons:
The partnership is the outcome of a contract. Thus:
There must be at least 2 persons to enter into a contract to form a partnership. b) Minors cannot form a partnership firm as they are incompetent to enter into a contract but can be admitted to the benefits of a running firm. c) If these people intend to do banking business, the maximum number can be ten otherwise twenty for the other business.

Agreement: The relation of partnership arises from contract and not from status. Though the oral agreement is even acceptable in practice, written agreement is much more advisable as disputes can be resolved better with it.

Profit-sharing: The objective of the business is to make profits and distribute the same amongst partners. Any association initiated to do charity work is not a partnership.

Unlimited liability: Mostly, the liability of the partners of a firm is unlimited. Their personal properties can be disposed of off to pay the debts of the firm if required. The creditors can claim their dues from any one of the partners or from all of them, meaning partners are liable:

- Individually
- Collectively

Implied authority: There is an implied authority that any partner can act on behalf of the firm. The firm stands bound by the acts of partners.

Mutual agency: The business of partnership can be carried on by all the partners or any one of them acting for all. Thus, every partner is principal as well as an agent of other partners and of the firm. Thus, **(i) Each partner is liable for acts performed by other partners, (ii) Each partner can bind other partners and the firm by his acts done in the ordinary course of business**.

Utmost good faith: Every partner is supposed to act honestly and give proper accounts to other partners. Thus, mutual faith and confidence in one another is the main strength of the partnership.

Restriction on transfer of shares: No partner can sell or transfer his share to anybody else without the consent of the other partners. By giving notice for the dissolution of the firm, a partner can show intention to discontinue as a partner. 9) Continuity: A partnership continues up to the time that all partners desire to continue it. Legally, a firm dissolves on the retirement, death, bankruptcy lunacy, or disability of a partner if not otherwise provided for in the partnership deed.

Suitability of Partnership

The use of better-sophisticated production techniques has necessitated more investments. The complex nature of businesses needs expert managerial hands. Thus, partnership form of a business is an ideal choice for starting a new venture, if the entrepreneurs–
capital and managerial requirements are higher as compared to that of a sole proprietorship, enterprise falls in the category of either being a small or a medium scale enterprise, direct contact with the customers is essential

Consequences for non–registration of a partnership firm

Partnership firms in India are governed by the Indian Partnership Act, 1932. While it is not compulsory to register your partnership firm as there are no penalties for nonregistration, it is advisable since the following rights are denied to an unregistered firm:

- A partner cannot file a suit in any court against the firm or other partners for the enforcement of any right arising from a contract or right conferred by the Partnership Act.

- A right arising from a contract cannot be enforced in any Court by or on behalf of the firm against any third party.
- Further, the firm or any of its partners cannot claim a set-off (i.e. mutual adjustment of debts owed by the disputant parties to one another) or other proceedings in a dispute with a third party.

Partnership deed

Meaning: Partnership is an agreement between persons to carry on a business, entered into either orally or in writing.
- It is always desirable to have a written agreement so as to avoid misunderstandings and unnecessary litigations in the future.
- When the agreement is in written form, it is called a 'Partnership Deed'.
- It must be duly signed by the partners, stamped, and registered.

Any alteration in one partnership deed can be made with the mutual consent of all the partners.

Registration procedure

Step 1: Application for partnership registration should include the following information:
- Name of the firm
- Name of the place where business is carried on
- Names of any other place where business is carried on
- Date of partners joining the firm
- Full name and permanent address of partners.
- Duration of the fir

Step 2: Every partner needs to verify and sign the application. Ensure that the following documents and prescribed fees are enclosed with the registration application. a) Application for registration in the prescribed form-I. b) Duly filled specimen of affidavit c) Certified copy of the partnership deed d) Proof of ownership of the place of business or the rental/lease agreement thereof.

Common limitations of sole proprietorship and partnership

- limited Resources and
- the limited life span of both sole proprietorship and partnership form of organization stands limited with
- liabilities being unlimited.

To comply with these growing needs, the demand was on rising for: 1) Capital 2) Managerial talent and skills 3) Limited liability Thus, the joint-stock company as a modern form of business organization emerged to meet the requirements of the large-sized businesses.

Joint Stock Company

In common prevalence, a company means a voluntary association of a person formed for some common object with capital divisible into units of equal value called 'shares' and with limited liability. Company is a creation of a law that is the birth of this artificial human being is by law and it can be put to death by law only. According to section 3 of the Indian companies act, 1956, "A company means a company formed and registered under this act or any previous act." Thus, a company is an association of persons who contribute money in the shape of shares and the company gets a legal entity and enjoys a permanent existence.

Characteristics of a Company: (VC-WALT-DSN)

Voluntary association: A single person cannot constitute a company. At least two persons, voluntarily, must join hands to form a private company, while a minimum of seven persons are required for a public company.

Artificial person: A company is created by law. Though it has no body and no conscience, it still exists as a person, having a distinct personality of its own. Because like a human being it can buy, sell and own property, sue others, be sued by others, its called as an artificial person.

Separate legal entity: A company has an independent status, different from its members. This implies that a company cannot be held liable for the actions of its members and vice-versa. The company has a distinct entity separate from its members.

Common seal: Being an artificial person, the company cannot sign the documents. Hence, it uses a common seal on which its name is engraved. Putting the common seal on papers, is equivalent to that of signatures of a human being, making them binding on the company.

Winding-up: The mode of incorporation and termination (winding up) is both as per the Companies Act only. It's born out of law and can be liquidated only by law.

The choice to be made

An entrepreneur, under the 'Company' form of organization has a further choice to incorporate an enterprise either as either a:
1. Private company
2. Public company

1. **Private company**

A private company:

- has a minimum of two and a maximum of 200 members excluding its past and present employees.
- restricts the right of its members to transfer shares.

prohibits an invitation to the public to subscribe for any shares or debentures of the company, or accept any deposits from persons other than its directors, members or relatives. has a minimum paid-up capital of one lakh rupees (subject to change) uses the word 'Pvt. Ltd.' at the end of its name.

2. **Public company**: Under Section 3(i) (ii) of the Companies Act, a public company is a company which is not a private company. By implication, a public company:
- has a minimum of seven people to commence with no upper limit to membership
- does not restrict any transfer of shares
- invites the public to subscribe for its shares, debentures, and public deposits.
- has a minimum paid-up capital of five lakh rupees.

Why the private company is more desirable (privileges)

- Only two members are required to form a private company.
- Only two directors are required to constitute the quorum to validate the proceedings of the meetings.
- Such a company can file a statement in lieu of a prospectus with the Registrar of Companies.
- It can commence its business immediately after incorporation.
- Holding of a statutory meeting or filing of a statutory report is required by a private company.
- A non-member cannot inspect the copies of the profit and loss A/c filed with the Registrar.
- Limit on payment of maximum managerial remuneration does not apply to a private company.
- Restrictions on appointment and reappointment of managing director do not apply. 9) Maintaining of the index of members is not required by a private company.
- Directors of the private company need not have qualification shares. The company form of organization has shown a phenomenal increase in almost all countries of the world in the twentieth century.

Suitability

- Venture is a heavy and basic industry type
- Large-scale operations are involved
- Business requires huge funds
- Enterprise involves heavy risks

Enterprise is technologically complex and sophisticated, banking heavily upon experts and professionals

To commence a "Company" in India

Promoters: The idea of forming a company is conceived either by a person or by a group of persons known as promoters. Our entrepreneurs are basically the promoters as they are the ones who:

- Conceive the idea.
- Scan it against the environmental forces to establish its feasibility and viability.
- Procures the resources essential for its commencement.
- Ensure the incorporation of the enterprise.
- Arrange for commencing of the business.
- Plans out expansion and diversification strategies

Important Point

The concept of the company is born in the entrepreneur's mind – they investigate the potential and take a lead for bringing human resources, money, materials, machinery, and methods together for converting his/her dream into reality.

Stages for the formation of a Company

- Stage 1: Promotion stage
- Stage 2: Incorporation stage
- Stage 3: Capital Subscription
- Stage 4: Commencement of business

Private companies can start their business after Stage 2: Incorporation stage because they don't have to issue shares to the general public. A public company can start a business only after completing all the four stages

Legal formalities are expected to be complied by the entrepreneur:

1. **Obtain PAN number from Income Tax Department**: Permanent Account Number (PAN) is a ten-digit alphanumeric number, issued by the Income Tax Department.

- PAN enables the department to link all transactions of the —person with the department. These transactions include tax payments, TDS/TCS credits, returns of income/wealth/ gift/FBT, specified transactions, correspondence, and so on. PAN, thus acts as an identifier for the —person with the tax department. It is mandatory to quote PAN in all documents pertaining to financial transactions.
- All existing assesses or taxpayers, ii) Any person carrying on any business or profession whose total sales, turnover, or gross receipts are or is likely to exceed five lakh rupees in any previous year: The Assessing Officer may allot PAN to any person either on his/her own or on a specific request from such person.

2. **Open current account i):** Any person, competent to contract and satisfactorily introduced to the Bank may open an account in his/her own name. He/she may not open more than one such account. Accounts may be opened in the names of two or more persons and may be made payable to. ii) Accounts can be opened for sole proprietorship firms, partnership firms, private limited and public limited companies, Joint Hindu families, trusts, clubs, associates, etc. satisfactorily introduced to the Bank and on fulfilling laid down procedures and tendering required credentials. iii) Accounts can be opened by minors of 14 years and above, if able to read and write, in their sole names.

Name of the business entity

Register for e-filing at MCA (Ministry of Corporate Affairs) portal 3. Apply for Director Identification Number (DIN) 4. Obtain Digital Signature Certificate (DSC) 5. Register DSC at MCA website 6. Apply for approval of the name of the company 7. Formulate Memorandum of Association 8. Formulate Articles of Association 9. Verify, stamp and sign Articles of Association 10. Verify the various forms required for incorporation of the company.

- **Register for service tax:** Service tax is, as the name suggests, a tax on Services. It is a tax levied on the transaction of certain services specified by the Central Government under the Finance Act, 1994. It is an indirect tax (akin to Excise Duty or Sales Tax), which means that normally, the service provider pays the tax and recovers the amount from the recipient of taxable service.
- **Register for VAT/sales tax Value added tax (VAT):** VAT is a multi-point destination-based system of taxation, with tax being levied on value addition at each stage of transaction in the production/ distribution chain. · The term 'value addition' implies the increase in value of goods and services at each stage of production or transfer of goods and services. · VAT is a tax on the final consumption of goods or services and is ultimately borne by the consumer Imp. Point: For identification/registration of dealers under VAT, the Tax Payer's Identification Number (TIN) is used. TIN consists of 11 digit numerals throughout the country. Its first two characters represent the State Code and the set-up of the next nine characters can vary in different States.
- **Excise duty:** Excise duty is a tax on the manufacture or production of goods. Excise duty on alcohol, alcoholic preparations, and narcotic substances is collected by the State Government and is called "State Excise" duty. The Excise duty on the rest of goods is called "Central Excise" duty and is collected in terms of Section 3 of the Central Excise Act, 1944. Sales Tax is different from the Excise duty as the former is a tax on the act of sale while the latter is a tax on the act of manufacture or production of goods. Customs duty is a type of indirect tax levied on goods imported either in or to India, not both, as well as on goods exported from India.
- **File entrepreneurship memorandum at DIC:** Although not mandatory, you may file part I of the entrepreneurs memorandum to the district industries center. This may be necessary for claiming certain incentives/subsidies and for certain formalities at the state level.
- **Apply for TAN:** TAN or tax deduction and collection account number is a 10 digit alphanumeric number required to be obtained by all persons who are responsible for deducting or collecting tax.
- **Post clearance:** Building completion/drainage completion/tree plantation certificate · Permission for mortgage · NOC from Pollution Control Board · Final fire clearance · NOC from environment department · Industrial safety permit · Sanction of permanent power · Sanction of permanent water and sewerage connection
- **Employee's Provident Fund (EPF):** Applicable for establishments employing 20 or more persons and engaged in the industry.
- **Employee's State Insurance (ESI) scheme:** The Act is applicable to non-seasonal factories employing 10 or more persons. The scheme has been extended to shops, hotels, restaurants, cinemas including preview theatres, road-motor transport undertakings, and newspaper establishments employing 20 or more persons.

A business plan is a document that defines in detail a company's objectives and how it plans to achieve its goals. A business plan lays out a written road map for the firm from marketing, financial, and operational standpoints. Both startups and established companies use business plans.

- A business plan is an important document aimed at a company's external and internal audiences. For instance, a business plan is used to attract investment before a company has established a proven track record. It can also help to secure lending from financial institutions.
- Furthermore, a business plan can serve to keep a company's executive team on the same page about strategic action items and on target for meeting established goals.
- Although they're especially useful for new businesses, every company should have a business plan. Ideally, the plan is reviewed and updated periodically to reflect goals that have been met or have changed. Sometimes, a new business plan is created for an established business that has decided to move in a new direction.

Understanding Business Plans

A business plan is a fundamental document that any new business should have in place prior to beginning operations. Indeed, banks and venture capital firms often require a viable business plan before considering whether they'll provide capital to new businesses.

- Operating without a business plan usually is not a good idea. In fact, very few companies are able to last very long without one. There are benefits to creating (and sticking to) a good business plan. These include being able to think through ideas before investing too much money in them and working through potential obstacles to success.
- A good business plan should outline all the projected costs and possible pitfalls of each decision a company makes. Business plans, even among competitors in the same industry, are rarely identical. However, they can have the same basic elements, such as an executive summary of the business and detailed descriptions of its operations, products and services, and financial projections. A plan also states how the business intends to achieve its goals.

Elements of a Business Plan

The length of a business plan varies greatly from business to business. Consider fitting the basic information into a 15- to 25-page document. Then, other crucial elements that take up a lot of space—such as applications for patents—can be referenced in the main document and included as appendices.

Executive summary: This section outlines the company and includes the mission statement along with any information about the company's leadership, employees, operations, and location.

Products and services: Here, the company can outline the products and services it will offer, and may also include pricing, product lifespan, and benefits to the consumer. Other factors that may go into this section include production and manufacturing processes, any patents the company may have, as well as proprietary technology. Information about research and development (R&D) can also be included here.

Market analysis: A firm needs a good handle on its industry as well as its target market. This section of the plan will detail a company's competition and how the company fits in the industry, along with its relative strengths and weaknesses. It will also describe the expected consumer demand for a company's products or services and how easy or difficult it may be to grab market share from incumbents.

Marketing strategy: This section describes how the company will attract and keep its customer base and how it intends to reach the consumer. A clear distribution channel must be outlined. The section also spells out advertising and marketing campaign plans and the types of media those campaigns will use.

Financial planning: This section should include a company's financial planning and projections. Financial statements, balance sheets, and other financial information may be included for established businesses. New businesses will include targets and estimates for the first few years plus a description of potential investors.

Budget: Every company needs to have a budget in place. This section should include costs related to staffing, development, manufacturing, marketing, and any other expenses related to the business.

Organizational Plan

Depicts the functional organizational (department hierarchy, for example) and reporting structures between the holders (employees or users) and positions to be filled (administrator in Sales) in an enterprise. In addition to this, it can include relationships between positions and tasks, jobs and work centers.

Structure

An organizational plan is made up of several separate hierarchies and catalogs that are related to one another. These hierarchies and catalogs are also consist of relationships between and lists of organizational objects . Thus, you can depict your enterprise in all its complexity.

Organizational structure: An organizational structure depicts the hierarchy in which the various organizational units at your enterprise are arranged. You create an organizational structure by creating and maintaining organizational units, and then creating relationships between the units.

Operational Plans

An operational business plan is a written document that describes the nature of the business, the sales and the marketing strategy which is optimal for success. It provides the vision, directions and goals for the organisation. An operational business plan is not a means to securing financing; however it is a good step-by-step guide to running your business in order to successfully create a product or service that will make it in the marketplace.

The operational business plan acts as a blueprint for your business processes which is an important guide to senior managers and other key stakeholders.

An operational business plan is like an orienteering map. The map helps you navigate to your destination using the easiest way possible and also guides you through certain obstacles and paths you may face. Without an orienteering map the chances of making it to the final destination are very slim and the process will be nothing but challenging and complex.

Purpose of Operational plans

The purpose of the business plan is to outline, in detail, the business's operation and future growth projections. It provides a framework that outlines the management approach and also ensures it covers many aspects relating to financial, marketing, staffing and other resources required to run a successful business. There are many reasons why a business should have an operational business plan. It helps the business move from start-up to success. It would be found that without this in place the business wouldn't be able to stay focused nor operate efficiently.

Type of Plan Created by Scope Includes Level of Detail

- Strategic Plan Top Management Entire organization Mission of the company, future goals and ambitions Very broad and general
- Tactical Plan Mid-level Management Single area of the business as a whole (e.g. a division of the company) Specific actions to support or work towards the Strategic Plan Specific actions and ideas, but not very detailed
- Operational Plan Low-level Management A unit within a single area of the business (e.g. a department within a division) Specific plans for low level and day-to-day activities and processes that will support and enable the Tactical Plan Extremely detailed (who, what, where and when).

Production Plan

Business success often hinges on making the products that customers want in a timely and cost-effective way. Production planning helps companies achieve those goals. It maps out all the processes, resources and steps involved in production, from forecasting demand to determining the raw materials, labor and equipment needed. Production planning helps companies build realistic production schedules, ensure production processes run smoothly and efficiently, and adjust operations when problems occur.

A production plan describes in detail how a company's products and services will be manufactured. It spells out the production targets, required resources, processes and overall schedule. The plan also maps all of the operational steps involved and their dependencies. The goal is to design the most efficient way to make and deliver the company's products at the desired level of quality. A well-designed production plan can help companies increase output and save money by developing a smoother workflow and reducing waste.

- Production planning describes in detail how a company's products and services will be manufactured.
- A production plan defines the production targets, required resources and overall schedule, together with all the steps involved in production and their dependencies.
- A well-designed production plan helps companies deliver products on time, reduce costs and respond to problems.
- Technology has made it easier for small and midsize companies in multiple industries to use production planning to optimize operations.

Types of Production Planning

The design of a product plan depends on the production method that the company uses, as well as other factors, such as product type, equipment capabilities and order size. Here are three of the main types of production planning:

Batch production planning: Refers to manufacturing identical items in groups rather than one at a time or in a continuous process. For some businesses, batch production can greatly increase efficiency. A bakery creating items for sale the next day might first make a batch of chocolate chip cookies, then move on to oatmeal raisin cookies followed by loaves of semolina bread. A clothing manufacturer making goods for the summer might first set up its cutting and sewing machines to make 500 navy-blue T-shirts, then switch to red fabric and thread to make 400 tank tops. A good production plan for batch processing should look out for potential bottlenecks or delays when switching between batches.

Job- or project-based planning: Used by many small- and medium-sized businesses, job production planning focuses on the creation of a single item by one person or team. Job-based planning is typically used where the specificity of each client's requirements means it is difficult to make products in bulk. Many construction businesses use this method. Makers of custom jewelry and dresses are other examples of businesses that may use job production planning.

Flow production planning: In flow production, also known as continuous production, standardized items are continuously mass-produced on an assembly line. Large manufacturers use this method to create a constant stream of finished goods. During production, each item should move seamlessly from one step along the assembly line to the next. Flow production is most effective at reducing costs and delays when there's steady demand for the company's products. Manufacturers can then readily determine their needs for equipment, materials and labor at each stage along the assembly line to help streamline production and avoid delays. The automotive industry and makers of canned foods and drinks are among the companies that use this method.

Financial Plan

A financial plan acts as the backbone for various aspects of the business. It focuses on long–term financial growth of the business. While setting up future targets, three aspects are considered: previous performance, revenue, and business valuation. These are crucial in the preparation and prediction of financial planning. The structure of a financial plan depends on strategy and execution. The financial plan clarifies the upcoming vision for growth. It detects potential complications, offers solutions, and analyses ways to stand out from the competition.

Objectives of a Financial Plan

Ample of funds: Before planning financial goals, a company or firm should ensure the sourcing of funds. Prior calculation of funds delivers a figure to achieve while making a financial plan.

Coverage to investors: There must be support for investors in the financial plan. Coverage can be achieved by balancing the risks and costs of the business. As investors contribute an amount and hold shares, they are accountable for every aspect of the financial plan.

Adjustable plans: The nature of business is dynamic and unpredictable. No one can predict the next trend, jump or dip in businesses. The plan should be formulated keeping this point in mind. It must be flexible and reformulated or modified according to the situation.

Less complicated: The financial plan should be easy to understand. Fewer securities make it actionable and adjustable for both users and investors.

Characteristics of a Financial Plan

Clear to the point: The financial plan should be clear at every point; less complex plans acquire more profit for the business. The wholesome objective of the business should be kept in mind while forming the structure. The sole target must be gaining funds and the support of investors. Along with growth and monetary profit, the plan should allocate equal focus to goodwill performance in the marketplace.

Less outsourcing: The structure of a financial plan should be independent of restrictions and outside funds. The beginning phase may acquire outside funds for foundation building, but the business should generate passive income afterwards. Passive income can be used efficiently and effectively for businesses.

Tentative: The formation of a financial plan should be flexible and adjustable. If any opportunities or critical situations come up, the plan should be soft and profitable at the same time. The main aim of planning is to attain profitability and stability in business. A financial plan must review short-term investments for less risk. Tentative financial plans build the capacity to face the challenges of the market.

Money-making: The plan should be profitable in every way. In the beginning, solely acquiring high profit may be ideal, but afterwards, the plan must reach profit goals. It must form a balance of insecurities to form a roadmap for movement towards high-profit goals.

Marketing Plan

A marketing plan is an operational document that outlines an advertising strategy that an organization will implement to generate leads and reach its target market. A marketing plan details the outreach and PR campaigns to be undertaken over a period, including how the company will measure the effect of these initiatives. The functions and components of a marketing plan include the following:

- Market research to support pricing decisions and new market entries

- Tailored messaging that targets certain demographics and geographic areas
- Platform selection for product and service promotion: digital, radio, Internet, trade magazines, and the mix of those platforms for each campaign
- Metrics that measure the results of marketing efforts and their reporting timelines

Types of Marketing Plans

There are a variety of different marketing plans that suit different businesses and different business needs.

New Product Launch: This is a marketing plan that outlines how a new product will enter the market, who it will target, and in what way advertising will be done.

Social Media: A social media marketing plan focuses on the advertising strategies on different social media platforms and how to engage with the users on these platforms.

Time-Based: Time-based marketing plans, such as those that are executed quarterly or annually, focus on the time of the year, the current condition of the business, and the best strategies in that period.

Human Resource Planning

Human resource planning (HRP) is the continuous process of systematic planning to achieve optimum use of an organization's most valuable asset—quality employees. Human resources planning ensures the best fit between employees and jobs while avoiding manpower shortages or surpluses.

There are four key steps to the HRP process. They include analyzing present labor supply, forecasting labor demand, balancing projected labor demand with supply, and supporting organizational goals. HRP is an important investment for any business as it allows companies to remain both productive and profitable.

Challenges of Human Resource Planning (HRP)

The challenges to HRP include forces that are always changing. These include employees getting sick, getting promoted, going on vacation, or leaving for another job. HRP ensures there is the best fit between workers and jobs, avoiding shortages and surpluses in the employee pool.

There are four general, broad steps involved in the human resource planning process. Each step needs to be taken in sequence in order to arrive at the end goal, which is to develop a strategy that enables the company to successfully find and retain enough qualified employees to meet the company's needs:

Analyzing labor supply: The first step of human resource planning is to identify the company's current human resources supply. In this step, the HR department studies the strength of the organization based on the number of employees, their skills, qualifications, positions, benefits, and performance levels.

Forecasting labor demand: The second step requires the company to outline the future of its workforce. Here, the HR department can consider certain issues like promotions, retirements, layoffs, and transfers—anything that factors into the future needs of a company. The HR department can also look at external conditions impacting labor demand, such as new technology that might increase or decrease the need for workers.

Balancing labor demand with supply: The third step in the HRP process is forecasting the employment demand. HR creates a gap analysis that lays out specific needs to narrow the supply of the company's labor versus future demand.

Goal of Human Resource Planning (HRP)

The goal of HR planning is to have the optimal number of staff to make the most money for the company. Because the goals and strategies of a company change over time, human resource planning must adapt accordingly. Additionally, as globalization increases, HR departments will face the need to implement new practices to accommodate government labor regulations that vary from country to country.

The increased use of remote workers by many corporations will also impact human resource planning and will require HR departments to use new methods and tools to recruit, train, and retain workers.

Multiple Choice Questions

1. Which one of the following actions by an entrepreneur is most likely to contribute to creative destruction?

   A. Development of a new product
   B. Take-over of a competitor
   C. Issuing shares
   D. Reducing prices

Answer: A

2. _________ advantage of the small firm in the innovation process.
   A. Ability to carry out R&D
   B. Ability to raise finance
   C. Ability of the entrepreneur to carry out multiple tasks
   D. Ability of the entrepreneur to act on new ideas or product development

Answer: D

Explanation:
Ability of the entrepreneur to act on new ideas or product development advantage of the small firm in the innovation process.

3. External links may provide incentives to:
   A. Raise finance
   B. Introduce new working practices
   C. Introduce improvements to products
   D. Attend business exhibitions

Answer: C

Explanation:
External links may provide incentives to Introduce improvements to products.

4. Firms located on science parks compared to those located off science parks are:
   A. More innovative
   B. Less innovative
   C. No more or less innovative
   D. More growth orientated

Answer: C

Explanation:
Firms located on science parks compared to those located off science parks are No more or less innovative.

5. Innovative small firms are more likely in:
   A. Knowledge-based sectors
   B. Biotechnology
   C. Automobile manufacture
   D. Aerospace manufacture

Answer: A

Explanation:
Innovative small firms are more likely in Knowledge-based sectors.

6. Schumpeter considered that innovative entrepreneurs would:
   A. Thrive
   B. Disappear
   C. Be absorbed within large innovative firms
   D. Be absorbed within non-innovative firms

Answer: C

Explanation:
Schumpeter considered that innovative entrepreneurs would Be absorbed within large innovative firms.

7. Innovative entrepreneurs face special issues in raising:
   A. Development capital
   B. Structured capital
   C. Human capital
   D. Seed capital

Answer: C

Explanation:
Innovative entrepreneurs face special issues in raising human capital.

8. Innovative entrepreneurs may have to pay high insurance premiums due to the:
   A. The need to protect patents
   B. Greater employee liability
   C. Greater customer liability
   D. Greater trading risks

Answer: A

Explanation:
Innovative entrepreneurs may have to pay high insurance premiums due to the the need to protect patents.

9. Networking by innovative entrepreneurs may be most encoura
   A. Science parksged by?
   B. Business incubators
   C. Chambers of Commerce
   D. Business associations

Answer: B

Explanation:

Entrepreneurial ecosystems and startup communities are environments that foster networking and collaboration among innovative entrepreneurs.

10. The most likely problem encountered by innovative entrepreneurs in raising finance is:

    A. Limited security since R&D is an intangible asset

    B. The costs of the patenting system

    C. The exhaustion of personal equity in R&D

    D. Inability of potential external funders to understand technology

Answer: C

Explanation:

The most likely problem encountered by innovative entrepreneurs in raising finance is the exhaustion of personal equity in R&D.

11. Which of the following is NOT recognized as a misconception about entrepreneurship?

    A. Successful entrepreneurship needs only a great idea.

    B. Entrepreneurship is easy.

    C. Entrepreneurship is found only is small businesses.

    D. Entrepreneurial ventures and small businesses are different.

Answer: D

Explanation:

Entrepreneurial ventures and small businesses are different is not recognized as a misconception about entrepreneurship.

12. All of the following are characteristics of small businesses EXCEPT:

    A. Small businesses are independently owned, operated, and financed.

    B. Small businesses have fewer than 100 employees.

    C. Small businesses emphasize new or innovative practices.

    D. Small businesses have little impact on industry.

Answer: C

Explanation:

All of the following are characteristics of small businesses EXCEPT Small businesses emphasize new or innovative practices.

13. Which of the following is NOT on of the three areas in which the importance of entrepreneurship can be shown?

    A. Innovation

    B. Number of new start-ups

    C. Job creation and employment

    D. bureaucracy

Answer: D

Explanation:

Bureaucracy is NOT on of the three areas in which the importance of entrepreneurship can be shown.

14. The creation of new firms is important because these new firms contribute to economic development through benefits that include all of the following EXCEPT:

    A. Product-process innovation

    B. Increased tax revenues

    C. Unemployment

    D. Social betterment

Answer: C

Explanation:

The creation of new firms is important because these new firms contribute to economic development through benefits that include all of the following EXCEPT Unemployment.

15. All of the following represent countries in which the highest level of entrepreneurial activity was found EXCEPT:

    A. Australia

    B. Korea

    C. Norway

    D. Japan

Answer: D

Explanation:

All of the following represent countries in which the highest level of entrepreneurial activity was found EXCEPT Japan.

16. Positive external trends or changes that provide unique and distinct possibilities for innovating and creating value are called __________.

    A. Strengths

    B. Opportunities

    C. Weaknesses

    D. Threats

Answer: B

Explanation:

Positive external trends or changes that provide unique and distinct possibilities for innovating and creating value are called Opportunities.

17. An individual who has no prior business ownership experience as a business founder, inheritor of a business, or a purchaser of a business is called a(n) __________ entrepreneur.

   A. Habitual   **B.** Novice

   C. Serial   **D.** Portfolio

Answer: B

Explanation:

An individual who has no prior business ownership experience as a business founder, inheritor of a business, or a purchaser of a business is called a(n) novice entrepreneur.

18. An individual who has prior business ownership experience is called a(n) __________ entrepreneur.

   A. Novice   **B.** Habitual

   C. Serial   **D.** Portfolio

Answer: B

Explanation:

An individual who has prior business ownership experience is called a Habitual entrepreneur.

19. All of the following are popular demographic factors about entrepreneurs that have been studied EXCEPT:

   A. Self-confidence   **B.** Gender

   C. Education   **D.** Family birth order

Answer: A

Explanation:

All of the following are popular demographic factors about entrepreneurs that have studied except self-confidence.

20. The three main responsibilities involved with managing an entrepreneurial venture once its up and running include all of the following EXCEPT:

   A. Managing processes   **B.** Managing people

   C. Managing bureaucracy   **D.** Managing growth

Answer: C

Explanation:

The three main responsibilities involved managing and entrepreneur venture when set up and running include managing process managing people and managing growth.

Chapter- 3   Enterprise Marketing

Introduction

Entrepreneurial marketing is a critical part of entrepreneurship that focuses on the customer as the fundamental driver of entrepreneurial success. As such, entrepreneurial marketers should not underestimate the importance of gathering customer insight to get new ideas, new products, and innovative processes.

Businesses that want to expand their companies often rely on specific marketing strategies to help them grow. Larger companies often use enterprise marketing strategies to meet business goals. Growing businesses and professionals in the business or marketing industries may benefit from learning about this complex marketing technique. In this article, we discuss what enterprise marketing is, common strategies, enterprise marketing tools, how to create an enterprise marketing strategy and tips for using it.

Enterprise marketing is a combination of multifaceted marketing strategies that emphasizes growth and expansion while retaining an existing customer base. An enterprise-level business is one that typically earns around one billion dollars in revenue per year and employs at least 1,000 people. Enterprise marketing may involve more than a company's internal marketing team to target audiences, the company may also use stakeholders, product developers and social media. The marketing team and additional contributors typically focus on sales promotions, public relations, content creation and social media besides advertising and working with stakeholders.

Marketing and Sales Strategy

Marketing strategy is defined by David Aaker as "a process that can allow an organization to concentrate its resources on the optimal opportunities with the goals of increasing sales and achieving a sustainable competitive advantage."

Without a strategy, all your Marketing and Sales activities and tactics might be for nothing. After all, if they don't all work in concert to drive pipeline and customer acquisition, what's the point? Savvy companies realize that a Sales and Marketing strategy is the next most important one after the overall business plan. It outlines how Sales and Marketing will orchestrate their efforts to achieve your key business goals, helping shape your organization's success and future.

Your Sales and Marketing strategy is your plan for reaching, engaging, and converting target prospects into profitable customers. It's the charter that guides Marketing and Sales in their daily activities, helping them clarify shared objectives and how to achieve them.

The Three Big Sales and Marketing Structural Gaps

The core of the problem is that Sales and Marketing are built to see the world differently. They consult their own sources for information, and follow different guidance when it comes to their targets and incentives.

Data Sets

It's no surprise that Sales and Marketing refer to different data sets – they use different technologies and tools to manage and track their activities and interactions with prospects and customers. While marketers use data management platform (DMP) and marketing automation systems, sales groups largely rely on customer relationship management (CRM) systems.

Marketing's number-one marching order is to generate and nurture leads. As a result, they're focused on sending large-scale campaigns aimed at generating leads and getting prospective buyers to raise their hands and move down the purchase path. The marketing data that indicates success is response rate and an optimal Cost Per Lead (CPL). Sales is focused on developing relationships with buyers to ultimately drive purchases. Sales success is reflected in data around pipeline health, forecasting accuracy, and closed deals. In other words, they speak different languages. Sales talks about pipelines, while marketing talks about funnels.

Target Audience

As described, Marketing and Sales have embraced different perspectives of the same world. This goes a long way toward explaining why it seems the two groups continue to butt heads and struggle to get on the same page. They don't even look at the target audience the same way. As a result, they miss out on a tone of valuable opportunities. Check out our earlier post for tips on arriving at a shared view of the target audience.

Given their different filters, it's no wonder opinions diverge in terms of how well the two groups are achieving important goals. As it drives a growing number of leads, Marketing believes it's exceeding its lead generation goals. Meanwhile, Sales is frustrated at a lack quality leads. In fact, sales folks routinely ignore 80% of marketing-generated leads due to lack of confidence in their colleagues' methods and information. Plus, both teams are missing many opportunities to connect with promising prospects. Imagine that 80% of your work as a marketer is going to waste!

Coordination

Due to these basic differences in how they're oriented and view their worlds, Sales and Marketing work in parallel rather than in tight collaboration. We're not saying animosity and adversity are par for the course between the two groups. In fact, many Sales and Marketing teams enjoy a friendly working relationship. They might even meet jointly to discuss and update buyer personas. In fact, they might feel the lead handoff goes smoothly. But that's often the best it gets…even though there's potential to do so much better.

While these three disconnects are no small matter, it is possible to close the gaps. It starts with a jointly developed strategy to connect with, engage, and convert today's buyers.

Features of marketing strategy:
- Marketing strategy includes all basic and long-term activities in the field of marketing that deal with the analysis of the strategic initial situation of a company.
- It also includes the formulation, evaluation and selection of market-oriented strategies and therefore contributes to the goals of the company and its marketing objectives.
- A marketing strategy is composed of several strategies for growth as well as interrelated components called the marketing mix.

Branding, Logo and Tagline

A brand is "a name, term, sign, symbol, or design or a combination of them which is intended to identify the goods or services of one seller or group of sellers and to differentiate them from those of the competitors."

A logo can be described as images, text or shapes that work to visually represent a business. A slogan however, is a series of words that summarise the purpose of a brand or to contextualise the personality of a brand.

A tagline is a phrase that highlights what a business does, emphasizes a value or specific message, and/or clarifies a brand's mission. You can think of taglines as a brand's mission statement condensed into a few words. It can be an important part of your brand's identity.

Branding

'Branding' is a process, a tool, a strategy, an orientation whereby a name, a sign, or a symbol, etc. is given to a product by the entrepreneur so as to differentiate his/her product from the rival products.

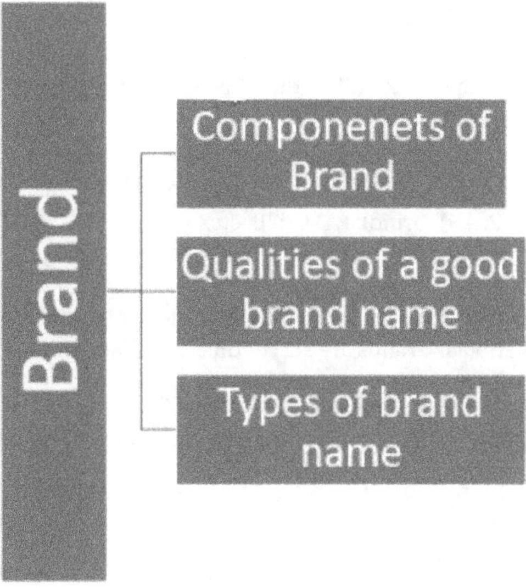

Importance/ Use/function of Brand

'Brand' is a comprehensive term. It is used to denote a name, term, sign, symbol, design or combination of them to:

- Identify the products of one firm, and
- Differentiate them from those of the competitors.

Components of Brand

Brand name: A brand name is "that part of a brand which can be vocalized i.e. can be spoken. It is like naming a newborn child. Mercedes, Woodland, Asian Paints, Pepsi, Maggie, Uncle Chips etc. are few examples of the brand names.

Brand mark: A brand mark is that part of a brand which can be recognized but cannot be vocalized i.e. is non-utterable. It appears in the form of a symbol, design or distinct colour scheme. For example: 'Girl' of Amul, 'Maharaja' of Air India, 'Ronald' of McDonald etc.

Trademark: A brand or part of a brand that is given legal protection against its use by other firms is called a trade mark. Thus, a trade mark is essentially a legal term, protecting the seller's exclusive right to use the brand name/mark.

Qualities of a good brand

While selecting a brand name, an entrepreneur should choose a name which is :

- Short, simple, and easy to pronounce.
- Noticeable, easy to recognize and remember.
- Pleasing, impressive when uttered.
- Neither obscene, negative, offensive or vulgar. e) Adaptable to packaging, labeling requirements, to different advertising media and languages.
- Linked to product, symbolically eye-catching.
- Contemporary, capable of being registered and protected legally

Brand management strategy

Brand management is a broad term used to describe marketing strategies to maintain, improve and bring awareness to the wider value and reputation of a brand and its products over time. A strong brand management strategy helps to build and nurture closer relationships with its audience.

Need of Brand management strategy:

The new product is given a name so that it can get public attention. Thus, as, the whole meaning and direction of a company can be explained through its brand management strategy, an entrepreneur should be very careful in deciding/in choosing its brand strategy.

Types of brand names available are:

Individual brand name: Here entrepreneur can choose distinct names for each of his offering, i.e. every product is promoted on the basis of a separate brand name. For example, Hindustan Unilever Ltd has emerged as the clear leader in the toilet soap industry and it has different brand name for different soaps, Lifebuoy, Liril, Lux.

Family brand name: Entrepreneur can opt to use a common or successful family name for their several products. Either the entrepreneur's name or the company's name may be used for all the products. It is even referred as Umbrella branding.

For example,(i) PONDS, is a mother brand name used for shampoos, talcum powder, cold creams, soaps, etc. (ii) MAGGI, is the brand name for noodles, sauces, masalas, etc. (iii) AMUL, has been used to market a large variety of dairy products viz. milk, ghee, butter, chocolates, etc.

- **Corporate names:** Entrepreneur can choose to utilise their corporate name or logo together with some brand names of individual products for example, Godrej, Tata, Bajaj, etc.
- **Alpha-numeric names:** In many industrial products, an alpha-numeric name often signifies its physical characteristics, thus creating a distinctive identity of the product. Entrepreneurs have an option available to brand his/her products alpha-numerically too. For example, SX4, Liv52, ANX Grindlay, i10, i20, etc.

Trademark

A trademark is a word, phrase, symbol or design, or a combination of them, that identifies and distinguishes the source of the goods of one party from those of others Popular brands are susceptible to imitation.

Thus, to be on the safer side, the entrepreneur should legally protect his/her brand name or mark through trademark. A trademark is meant to guard against ditto imitations. The best way for a new brand to succeed is to carry the mantle from the old brand, if any

Service mark

A service mark is a brand name or logo that identifies a business. Service marks can consist of words, phrases, symbols, designs, or some combination of these elements, which are all a form of intellectual property. Service marks identify a brand and the quality associated with it.

Logo

Logo is a distinctive design, mark, sign which stands associated with the entrepreneur's offering. ' Logos are either purely graphic (symbols/icons) or are composed of the name of the organization (a logotype or wordmark).

Purpose/ functions of Logo:(GIESK)

- Logos are a critical aspect of business marketing. As the company's major graphical representation, a logo anchors company's brand.
- Corporate Logos are intended to be the "Identity" of an enterprise because of displaying graphically the enterprise's uniqueness.
- Enterprises normally resort to logos' as a short path for advertising and other marketing materials.
- Logos act as the key visual component of an enterprise's overall brand identity.

Tagline

Taglines are basically simple but powerful messages that help to communicate an enterprise's goals, mission, distinct qualities and so much more. Thus, a 'tagline' is a small amount of text which serves to clarify a thought and is designed with a dramatic effect.

Packaging

Packaging is often the key element in assisting, mainly consumer goods companies, to achieve a comparative advantage. The critical decisions that must be made on the package are concerned with the functions, the product packaging will perform as well as with the mix of packaging components best able to perform in different degrees, the particular functions of the packaging.

Levels of packaging

There are three levels of packaging as discussed below:

- Primary package: Which encloses the actual commodity.
- Secondary package: which is the layer of cover added to the primary package for its product.
- Transportation package: It refers to further packaging components necessary for storage and transportation.

Labeling

It is the display of information about a product on its container, packaging, or the product itself. The label can be in the form of simple tags or computer graphics that are part of a package.

Functions/ Importance of labeling

Labeling is important because of the following reasons:

- It describes the product and specifies its content.
- It helps in the identification of the product or brands.
- It helps to grade the products.
- It helps in the promotion of the product.
- It helps in providing information as required by law.

Intellectual Property Rights

Intellectual property (IP) rights are the legally recognized exclusive rights to creations of the mind. Under this law, owners are granted certain exclusive rights to a variety of intangible assets.

Price and Pricing strategies/ Methods

Refers to the value that is put for a product. It is only the revenue-generating element among the 4Ps. The price of a product depends on cost of production, segment targeted, ability of the market to pay, supply – demand and a host of other direct and indirect factors.

Pricing

It involves the determination of the price of the product. It plays an important role in the marketing of goods and services.

Pricing strategies:

Cost-plus pricing:

The most common technique is cost-plus pricing, where the manufacturer charges a price to cover the cost of producing a product plus a reasonable profit. Cost-plus pricing is typically based on a manufacturing estimate. Manufacturing estimates are made of the resources required, the cost of these resources, and the time for which they will be used. On the basis of these estimates, the price is determined.

Estimates of the production cost are made to:

- justify planned capital expenditure
- determine likely production costs for new or modified products
- focus attention on areas of high cost

Advantages of cost-plus pricing

- Biggest advantage of this is that company knows exactly the amount of expenditure that has incurred on making a product and therefore they can add profit margin accordingly which helps in achieving the desired revenue for a firm.
- It is the simplest method to decide the price for a product.
- It helps in o evaluating the reasons for escalations in expenses and therefore it can take corrective action immediately.

Disadvantages of cost-plus pricing

- This method does not take into account the future demand for a product which should be the base before deciding on the price of a product
- It also does not take into account the competitors actions and their effect on pricing of the product,
- It can result in the company overestimating the price of a product because this method includes sunk cost and ignores opportunity cost also while calculating cost there is an element of personal bias while deciding the profit margin which is to be added to a product.

Penetration pricing

Penetration pricing is a pricing strategy where the price of a product is initially set at a price lower than the eventual market price to attract new customers. The price will be raised later once this market share is gained.

- The strategy works on the expectations that customers will switch to the new brand because of the lower price.
- Penetration pricing is most commonly associated with a marketing objective of increasing market share or sales volume, rather than to make profit in the short term.

Advantages of penetration pricing to the firm are:

- It can result in fast diffusion and adoption. This can achieve high market rates quickly. This can take the competitors by surprise, not giving them time to react.
- It can create goodwill among the early adopters segment. This can create more trade by word of mouth.
- It creates cost control and cost reduction pressures from the start, leading to greater efficiency.
- It discourages the entry of competitors. Low prices act as a barrier to entry · It can create high stock turnover throughout the distribution channel
- This can create critically important enthusiasm and support in the channel.

Disadvantages of penetration pricing

- It establishes long–term price expectations for the product and image preconceptions for the brand and company. This makes it difficult to eventually raise prices.

- Another potential disadvantage is that the low profit margins may not be sustainable long enough for the strategy to be effective.

Creaming or skimming

In this type of pricing strategy, entrepreneur set their prices higher so that fewer sales are needed to break even.

- Skimming is usually employed to reimburse the cost of investment of the original research into the product commonly used in electronic markets.
- This strategy is often used to target "early adopters" of a product or service who have a relatively lower price-sensitivity.
- it is generally bought by consumers who have a greater understanding of the product's value, or simply having a higher disposable income.
- This strategy is employed only for a limited duration to recover most of the investment made to build the product.

Advantages of skimming price

- Price skimming helps the company in recovering the research and development costs which are associated with the development of a new product.
- If the company caters to consumers who are quality conscious rather than price conscious, then this type of strategy can work in a great way for a company.

Disadvantages of skimming price

- This strategy can backfire if there are close competitors and they also introduce same products at lower price then consumers will think that the company always sells the products at higher prices.
- Price skimming is not a viable option when there are strict legal and government regulations regarding consumer rights.
- If the company has history of price skimming then consumers will never buy a product when it is newly launched, they would rather wait for a few months and buy the product at lower price.

Variable price method

Variable pricing is a marketing approach that permits different rates to be extended to different customers for the same goods or services. This approach is generally followed for businesses where bargaining over the price is the norm, as with street vendors. Also, this method is witnessed in the process of bidding or discounted price being offered in case of bulk purchases.

Advantages of variable pricing:

- Sellers can use this method of pricing to sell those goods and services that they have not been able to sell at original price.
- By selling their products at variable price, the sellers are able to earn a modest profit and recoup their investment in the product.

Disadvantages of variable pricing:

- It can lead to losing other consumers who paid full price for their purchase if they find out that another customer was able to purchase the same product at a lower price.
- Goodwill of the business is adversely affected.

Place mix (distribution)

A channel of distribution or trade channel is defined as the path or route along which goods move from producers or manufacturers to ultimate consumers or industrial users.

- It is a distribution network through which the producer puts his products in the market and passes it to the actual users.
- This channel consists of producers, consumers or users and the various middlemen like wholesalers, selling agents and retailers (dealers) who intervene between the producers and consumers.

Therefore, the channel serves to bridge the gap between the point of production and the point of consumption thereby creating time, place, and possession utilities.

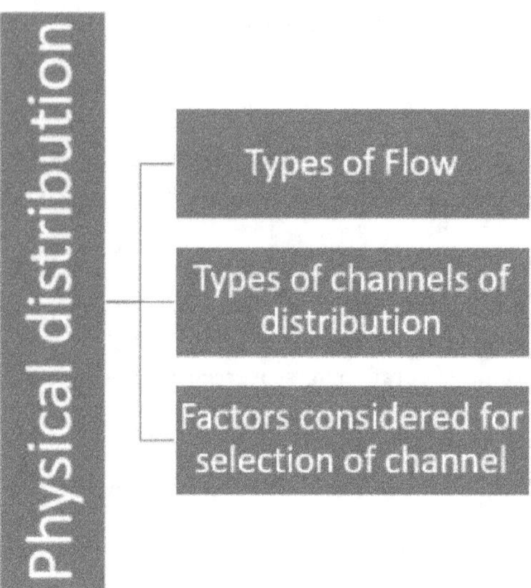

Types of channels of distribution

Producer-customer (Direct channel-zero level): This is the simplest and shortest channel in which no middlemen is involved and producers directly sell their products to the consumers.

Advantages
- It is fast and economical channel of distribution.
- Under it, the producer or entrepreneur performs all the marketing activities himself and has full control over distribution.
- A producer may sell directly to consumers through door-to-door sales persons, direct mail or through his own retail stores.
- Big firms adopt this channel to cut distribution costs and to sell industrial products of high value. Small producers and producers of perishable commodities also sell directly to local consumers.

Producer-retailer-customer (Indirect-one level):
This channel of distribution involves only one middleman called 'retailer'. Under it, the producer sells his/ her product to big retailers (or retailers who buy goods in large quantities) who in turn sell to the ultimate consumers.

Advantages: This channel relieves the manufacturer from burden of selling the goods himself and at the same time gives him control over the process of distribution.

Suitability: This is often suited for the distribution of consumer durables and products of high value.

Producer-agent-wholesaler-retailer-customer (Three levels): This is the longest channel of distribution in which three middlemen are involved. This is used when the producer wants to be fully relieved of the problem of distribution and thus hands over his/her entire output to the selling agents. The agents distribute the product among a few wholesalers. Each wholesaler distributes the product among a number of retailers who finally sell it to the ultimate consumers.

Suitability: This channel is suitable for the wider distribution of various industrial products.

Qualities of a good channel of distribution: An entrepreneur has to choose a suitable channel of distribution for his/her product such that the channel chosen is flexible, effective and consistent with the declared marketing policies and programmes of the firm.

Factors affecting channels of distribution:

While selecting a distribution channel, the entrepreneur should compare the costs, sales volume and profits expected from alternative channels of distribution and take into account the following factors:

Considerations related to product: When a manufacturer selects some channel of distribution he/she should take care of such factors which are related to the quality and nature of the product. They are as follows:

Unit value of the product : When the product is very costly it is best to use a small distribution channel. On the other hand, for less costly products long distribution channel is used.

Standardised or customised product: Standardised products are those for which cost is pre-determined and there is no scope for alteration. To sell this long distribution channel is used. On the other hand, customised products are those which are made according to the discretion of the consumer and also there is a scope for alteration,. For such products face-to-face interaction between the manufacturer and the consumer is essential. So for these direct sales is a good option.

Perishability: A manufacturer should choose minimum or no middlemen as channel of distribution for such an item or product which is of highly perishable nature. On the contrary, a long distribution channel can be selected for durable goods.

Technical nature: If a product is of technical nature, then it is better to supply it directly to the consumer. This will help the user to know the necessary technicalities of the product.

Considerations related to market:

Number of buyers: If the number of buyers is large then it is better to take the services of middlemen for the distribution of the goods. On the contrary, the distribution should be done by the manufacturer directly if the number of buyers is less.

Types of buyers: Buyers can be of two types: General Buyers and Industrial Buyers. If the more buyers of the product belong to general category then there can be more middlemen. But in case of industrial buyers there can be fewer middlemen.

Buying habits: A manufacturer should take the services of middlemen if his/her financial position does not permit him/her to sell goods on credit to those consumers who are in the habit of purchasing goods on credit.

Buying quantity: It is useful for the manufacturer to rely on the services of middlemen if the goods are bought in smaller quantity.
Size of market: If the market area of the product is scattered fairly, then the producer must take the help of middlemen.

Considerations related to manufacturer/company

Considerations related to the manufacturer are given below:

Goodwill: Manufacturers' goodwill also affects the selection of channels of distribution. A manufacturer enjoying a good reputation need not depend on the middlemen as he can open his own branches easily.

Desire to control the channel of distribution: A manufacturer's ambition to control the channel of distribution affects its selection. Consumers should be approached directly by such type of manufacturer. For example, the electronic goods sector with a motive to control the service levels provided to the customers at the point of sale is resorting to company-owned retail counters.

Financial strength: A company that has a strong financial base can evolve its own channels. On the other hand, financially weak companies would have to depend upon middlemen.

Considerations related to government

Considerations related to the government also affect the selection of channels of distribution. For example, only a license holder can sell medicines in the market according to the law of the government. In this situation, the manufacturer of medicines should take care that the distribution of his product takes place only through such middlemen who have the relevant license.

Promotion Strategy

This refers to all the activities undertaken to make the product or service known to the user and trade.

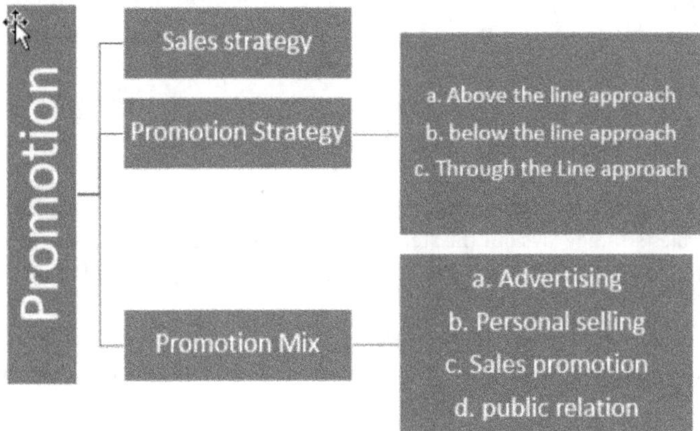

Sales Strategy

A sales strategy consists of a plan that positions a company's brand or product to gain a competitive advantage. Successful strategies help the sales force focus on target market customers and communicate with them in relevant and meaningful ways.

Significance of sales strategy

Creating awareness about the business environment: Planning and creating an effective sales strategy requires looking at long-term sales goals and analyzing the business sales cycle, as well as meeting with sales people about their personal career goals. Going through these exercises helps business owners and managers gain a more intimate knowledge of the sales intervals, seasonal changes and what motivates the sales team.

Helps in measuring the short-term performance of sales team: After creating the long-term sales strategy based on long-term goals, sales managers should create monthly and weekly sales strategies based on the long-term strategy. This allows for short-term performance measurement of the sales team.

Types of sales strategy

Businesses employ one of two basic types of sales strategies to their overall plan:

- Direct sales strategy
- Indirect sales strategy

Direct sales strategy/ Negative Selling: With the direct sales strategy, sales people attack the competition head on when talking to the customer. They talk about each feature of the competition's product and compare it to theirs. The term "negative selling" refers to the direct sales approach.

Indirect sales strategy/ Positive Selling: Indirect sales approaches apply more subtle techniques by demonstrating features and benefits not available with the competition's products or services without ever mentioning them by name. This more sophisticated, positive sales strategy requires research and analysis of the competition.

Component of sales strategy

Product Placement: Private placement is basically an advertising technique used by companies to certainly promote their products through a non traditional advertising technique. usually through appearance in film television or other media. yes for example Coca Cola could pay a given see to have the main lead of film drinking coke instead of Pepsi or farhan Akhtar driving Royal Enfield bike in "bhag milkha bhag"

Promotion: Promotion refers to this goes on all such activities with intent to inform customers about the products of the company and persuade them to buy these products. promotion makes use of various tools like advertising ,personal selling, sales promotion and public relations to encourage exchange of goods and services in the market .

Testimonials: Business should make use of social media networks like Facebook and Twitter to communicate with their customers. customer testimonials and feedback should regularly be posted on the companies site and should be readily available for prospects to read or watch. this lens authenticity to the claim made by a business with regards to its products or services.

Core Selling Strategies: There are a number of strategies available for the sales personnel to carry out their responsibilities and duties effectively but the success of these strategies depends on the identification and analysis of those factors that are treated as drivers of selling strategy formulation. some of the common drivers of selling strategies are:

- Tapping unconventional market
- Niche marketing
- Product positioning
- Making use of core competencies
- Customer services
- Corporate image
- Technological leadership etc.

Functions of sales strategy

The main two functions of sales strategy are given below:

New customer approach: A sales strategy lays out the steps and methods necessary for customers in different stages. Potential customers need communication that introduces the brand and product or service in ways that show how it can solve his or her problems.

Customer retention: Current customers require more personal communication about new features or benefits to keep them engaged. Promotions and referral discounts work to motivate current customers to spend their money and to spread the word to others.

Considerations while formulating sales strategy

Small business owners wishing to create and implement a sales strategy for the first time may want to hire a professional business consultant to help guide the process. Creating an effective sales strategy requires:

- Market knowledge,
- Awareness of competitor activities
- Awareness of current trends and
- Detailed business analysis.

Promotion strategy

Promotion is the method to spread the word about the product or service to customers, stakeholders and the broader public. Promotion strategy is a comprehensive plan that aims at finding an appropriate market for a product or service utilizing all aspects of promotion such as advertising and discounts used to promote the product or service in a particular market.

There are various approaches a company can use to promote its products viz.,

1. Above-the-line (ATL)
2. Below-the-line (BTL)
3. Through-the-line (TTL)

Various approaches of Promotion:
Above-the-line: Above-the-line promotions use mass media methods. This type of promotion focuses on advertising to a large audience. It includes conventional media like print, online, television and cinema advertising advertisements in the press. online banner advertisements, place advertisements on billboards and use their website to meet the needs of their consumers.

Advantage:
The advantage of following this approach of promotion is that it has a very broad reach and is largely uncarpeted.

Disadvantage:
- Making a message memorable to a large audience is not always easy.
- It is difficult to tailor a promotion to a specific group of consumers through above-the-line promotions. This is because it is viewed by a mass audience with different tastes and needs.
- Above-the-line promotion is also very expensive.

Below-the-line: Below-the-line methods are very specific, memorable activities focused on targeted groups of consumers. They are under the control of the organisation. The purpose of these activities has been to develop the brand by creating awareness and building a brand profile, which include:
- sponsorship
- sales promotions
- public relations
- personal selling
- direct marketing

Advantages
- this approach facilitates in building customer relationship
- lower investment is required
- promotion can be extremely targeted which results in a better response rate.

Disadvantages
- Targeting may be difficult
- Extensive training may be required for marketing teams
- customers may not trust the one to one contact due to earlier negative experiences.
- targeting the diverse cultures and users with the same theme is difficult.

Through-the-line:
Through the line" refers to an advertising strategy involving both above-and below-the line communications in which one form of advertising points the target to another form of advertising thereby crossing the "line".

Difference between above the line (ATL) and below the line (BTL)

Bases	Above the line	Below the line
Target	Mass audience	Identified small groups
Promotions	Establishing brand identity	Can lead to an actual sale
Measurability	Difficult to measure	Easy to measure
Examples	Print, online, television and cinema advertising	Sponsorship, sales promotions, public relations, personal selling, direct marketing

Promotion Mix
Once we have identified the target market, we have to think of the best way to reach them, but most businesses use a mix of advertising, personal selling, referrals, sales promotion, and public relations to promote their products or services.
- Advertising
- Personal Selling
- Sales Promotion
- Public Relations

Promotion Mix

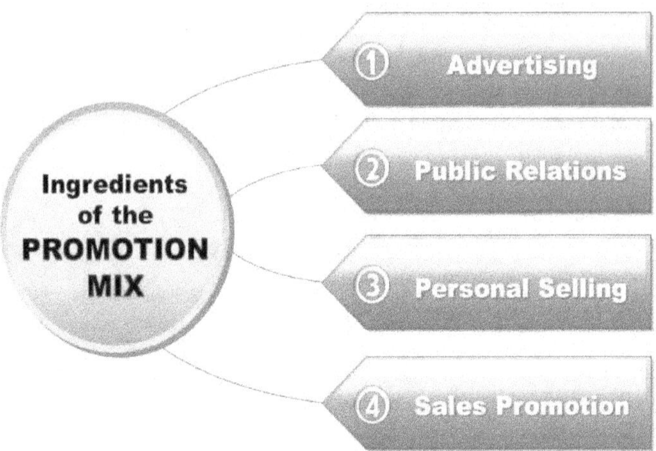

Advertising

Advertising is a paid form of communication designed to persuade potential customers to choose the product or service over that of a competitor.

Quality/ feature of advertising: It should be a planned, consistent activity that keeps the name of the business and the benefits of products or services uppermost in the mind of the consumer.

Objectives of Advertising

The objective of advertising is to increase profit by increasing sales. Advertising aims to:
- Make business and product name familiar to the public
- Create goodwill and build a favourable image
- Educate and inform the public
- Offer specific products or services
- Attract customers to find out more about your product or service.

Developing Effective Advertising (AIDA)

Good advertising generally elicits the following four responses:
- Attention – It catches the eye or ear and stands out amid the clutter of competing advertisements.
- Interest – It arouses interest and delivers sufficient impact in the message or offering.
- Desire – It creates a desire to learn more or crave ownership.
- Action – It spurs an action which leads to achievement of the ad's original objective – i.e. it prompts potential customers to purchase or use your product or service.

Personal selling

It means selling products personally. It involves the oral presentation of a message in the form of conversation with one or more prospective customers for the purpose of making sales.

Features of personal selling:
- It is personal form of selling.
- It leads to development of relations
- It has a narrow coverage
- It has the features of flexibility

Roles of a salesperson: Companies appoint salespeople to contact prospective buyers and create awareness about the company's product.

Thus a salesperson plays three different roles:
- Be persuasive
- A service provider
- Be informative

Sales promotion/ below the line activities

Sales promotion relates to short–term incentives or activities that encourage the purchase or sale of a product or service. Sales promotions initiatives are often referred to as —below the line‖ activities.

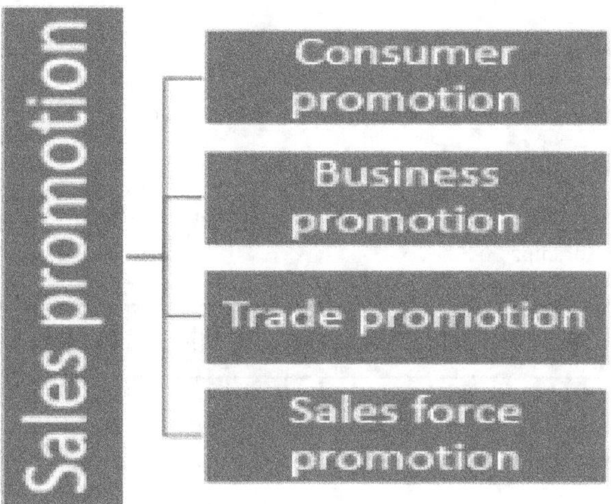

The major sales promotion activities:

Consumer promotions: Sales promotion activities targeted towards final buyers are called consumer promotions activities.

Business promotions:

- Seminars and workshops
- Conference presentations

Trade Promotions: Reward incentives linked to purchases or sales

Sales Force Promotions:

Public Relations

It is the deliberate, planned and sustained effort to establish and maintain mutual understanding between an organisation (or individual) and its (or their) public.

- Public relations is about building good relations with the stakeholders (public) of the business by obtaining favourable publicity, building a good corporate image and handling or heading off unfavourable rumours, stories and events.
- By building good relationships with the stakeholders, particularly customers, we can generate positive word of mouth and referrals from satisfied customers.

Stakeholder

Stakeholders are the various groups in a society which can influence or pressure your business decision making and have an impact on its marketing performance.

These groups include:

- Clients/customers
- Staff Shareholders
- Strategic partners
- Media Government

- Local community
- Financial institutions, Community groups

The main public relations tools:
Typical public relations tools include:
- News creation and distribution (media releases)
- Special events such as news conferences, grand openings and product launches
- Speeches and presentations
- Educational programs
- Annual reports, brochures, newsletters, magazines and Audio–visual presentations
- Community activities and sponsorships

Multiple Choice Questions

1. Which of these is true about marketing?

    A. Marketing is used to promote the product and services

    B. Marketing is concerned about the sales only

    C. Marketing is the activity, set of institutions, and processes for creating, communicating, delivering, and exchanging offerings that have value for customers, clients, partners, and society at large.

    D. Marketing considers only the needs of the organization and not the society

Answer: C

Explanation:

Marketing is the activity, set of institutions, and processes for creating, communicating, delivering, and exchanging offerings that have value for customers, clients, partners, and society at large. Marketing is the activity, set of institutions, and processes for creating, communicating, delivering, and exchanging offerings that have value for customers, clients, partners, and society at large.

2. Which one is not a part of the 4 Ps?

    A. Product

    B. People

    C. Price

    D. Place

Answer: B

Explanation:

People are a part of the 7 Ps. The concept of the 7 Ps is used in service marketing. The 4 Ps are product, price, place, and promotion.

3. Who is the Father of Modern Marketing?

    A. Philip Kotler

    B. Peter F Drucker

    C. Abraham Maslow

    D. Raymond Kroc

Answer: A

Explanation:

Philip Kotler is the father of modern marketing. He is an American marketing author and professor emeritus.

4. _____________defined marketing as the science and art of exploring, creating, and delivering value to satisfy the needs of a target market at a profit.

    A. Steve Jobs

    B. Philip Kotler

    C. Peter Drucker

    D. Abraham Maslow

Answer: B

Explanation:

Philip Kotler defined marketing as the science and art of exploring, creating, and delivering value to satisfy the needs of a target market at a profit.

5. The term "Marketing" refers to?

    A. Promotion of the product

    B. Focusing on sales and profit

    C. Strategizing and implementing the organization process

    D. Set of activities to deliver customer value and satisfaction

Answer: D

Explanation:

The term "Marketing" refers to Set of activities to deliver customer value and satisfaction.

6. _______________ is the key term in AMA's definition of marketing?

A.	Sales	**B.**	Promotion
C.	Value	**D.**	Profit

Answer: C

Explanation:

In its standard definition of marketing, the American Marketing Association focuses on Value to the customers.

7. Why must the marketers monitor the competitor's activities?

A.	The competitor may destroy the organization	**B.**	The competitor may threaten the monopoly position of the company
C.	New offerings of a competitor may need alterations in one or more components of the company's marketing mix	**D.**	The competitor may be violating the law to gain an advantage

Answer: C

Explanation:

New offerings of a competitor may need alterations in one or more components of the company's marketing mix must the marketers monitor the competitor's activities.

8. Different price points for a different level of quality for a company's related products is a part of which pricing strategy?

A.	Product line pricing	**B.**	Incremental pricing
C.	Optional product pricing	**D.**	By-product pricing

Answer: A

Explanation:

In product line pricing the company adds features to the base product and charges more for the features, as compared to the base product.

9. In today's time marketing must be understood and developed as?

A.	Getting the first mover's advantage	**B.**	Creating value for the customers
C.	Pushing for higher sales and profits	**D.**	Creating innovative products

Answer: B

Explanation:

The concept of marketing has evolved from production to creating value for the customers.

10. Which one of these is an appropriate definition of "want"?

A.	The desires of consumers	**B.**	Needs related to society
C.	Basic human needs	**D.**	Needs directed to the product

Answer: D

Explanation:

When a buyer sees a gap or problem it is a need. Only when the buyer decides that his need can be fulfilled by a particular product does it become a want.

11. Simply Clever' is the tagline of which company or brand?

A.	BOSE	**B.**	Bosch
C.	KPMG	**D.**	Skoda

Answer: D

Explanation:

Simply Clever' is the tagline of skoda company or brand.

12. Delivering Lifestyle' is the tagline of which company or brand?

A.	Jabong	**B.**	Myntra
C.	Snapdeal	**D.**	Provoge

Answer: A

Explanation:

Delivering Lifestyle' is the tagline of Jabong company or brand.

13. 'Stay New' is the tagline of which company or brand?

A.	Samsung	**B.**	Ebay

    C. Gillette   **D.** Old Spice

Answer: A

Explanation:

'Stay New' is the tagline of Samsung company or brand.

14. 'Reinvent' is the tagline of which company or brand?

    A. Nestle   **B.** Lakme

    C. Garnier   **D.** Emami

Answer: B

Explanation:

'Reinvent' is the tagline of Lakme company or brand.

15. 'The Power of Dreams' is the tagline of which company or brand?

    A. Disney   **B.** Michelin

    C. Honda   **D.** Blackberry'

Answer: C

Explanation:

'The Power of Dreams' is the tagline of Honda company or brand.

16. Companies use _______ for the equity of a brand name to address segment needs.

    A. Brand element   **B.** Brand bonding

    C. Sub-brand   **D.** None of the above

Answer: C

Explanation:

Companies use sub-brand for the equity of a brand name to address segment needs.

17. If a company uses successful brand names to launch a new or modified product in a new category, this strategy is called _____.

    A. Brand extension   **B.** Co-branding

    C. Line extension   **D.** Multi branding

Answer: A

Explanation:

If a company uses successful brand names to launch a new or modified product in a new category, this strategy is called Brand extension.

18. The strategy adopted by retailers and wholesalers for creating their private brand is called _____.

    A. Store brand   **B.** Mega brand

    C. Brand extension   **D.** Co-brand

Answer: A

Explanation:

The strategy adopted by retailers and wholesalers for creating their private brand is called Store brand.

19. When two brand names from different companies use the name of the same product, this branding strategy is called ______.

    A. Umbrella branding   **B.** Store branding

    C. Mega branding   **D.** Co-branding

Answer: D

Explanation:

When two brand names from different companies use the name of the same product, this branding strategy is called Co- branding.

20. The strategy of using a name, logo, sign, symbol or design, etc. to help consumers identify a product or service, and also differentiate it from competitors is called _______.

    A. Umbrella branding   **B.** Branding

    C. Mega branding   **D.** Co-branding

Answer: B

Explanation:

The strategy of using a name, logo, sign, symbol or design, etc. to help consumers identify a product or service, and also differentiate it from competitors is called Branding.

Chapter - 4 Enterprise Growth Strategies

Introduction

In earlier chapters, we studied the initial phase of setting an entrepreneurial organization and putting systems and processes in place to run the business. The next big challenge comes for the entrepreneur in the form of growing the business through various strategies. Once the product or service hits the market and it gains acceptability then it needs to be expanded into new areas. Here the question comes, which strategy is better to adopt. Should it be Franchising, Merger, and Acquisition or self-driven? In this chapter, we will discuss this aspect of an entrepreneurial organization.

Franchising

A franchise is a license granted to an individual or business entity (the franchisee) to market a company's (the franchisor) product or service in a particular territory using the franchisor's business systems, trademarks, and methods of operation.

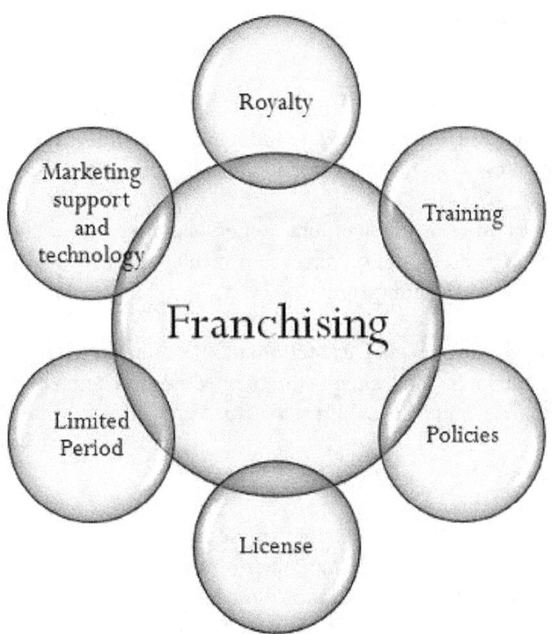

A franchise is a joint venture between a franchisor and a franchisee. The franchisor is the original business. It sells the right to use its name and idea. The franchisee buys this right to sell the franchisor's goods or services under an existing business model and trademark.

Franchises are a popular way for entrepreneurs to start a business, especially when entering a highly competitive industry such as fast food. One big advantage to purchasing a franchise is you have access to an established company's brand name. You won't need to spend resources getting your name and product out to customers.

Franchise Basics and Regulations

Franchise contracts are complex and vary for each franchisor. Typically, a franchise agreement includes three categories of payment to the franchisor. First, the franchisee must purchase the controlled rights, or trademark, from the franchisor in the form of an upfront fee. Second, the franchisor often receives payment for providing training, equipment, or business advisory services. Finally, the franchisor receives ongoing royalties or a percentage of the operation's sales.

A franchise contract is temporary, akin to a lease or rental of a business. It does not signify business ownership by the franchisee. Depending on the contract, franchise agreements typically last between five and 30 years, with serious penalties if a franchisee violates or prematurely terminates the contract.

Franchising – Concept

All of us have heard of booming franchise business. Every other day we witness increasing number of franchise food chains or retail chains in malls or popular marketing hubs. A franchise is a right granted to an individual or group to market a company's goods or services within a certain territory or location.

In other words, when a company decides to distribute its products or services to an independent third party operator on a contract basis, it is known as franchise business. In today's cut-throat competition market everyone wants to stay ahead in the race. One of the ways to get an advantage over the competitors is by indulging in franchise business.

Franchisee is the independent third party operator using registered products and services whereas the company that grants the rights to the franchisee to use its products and techniques. The best contribution of franchises is in developing independent entrepreneurs who want to be their own boss. There are plenty of franchise businesses available worldwide which are being operated by self-driven individuals.

The terms and conditions of agreement vary widely. But generally, the franchiser agrees to maintain a continuing interest in such areas of the franchisee's business as site selection, staff training, financing, marketing and promotion. He also allows the use of his brand or trade name, and standard operating procedure. In return, the franchisee agrees to operate under the specified conditions.

There are four major types of franchises:

Business Format Franchises:

This is the most common type of franchise. Here a company expands by supplying an established business concept/format, including its brand name, symbol, and/or trademark to independent business owners. In this arrangement, the franchisee acquires the right to use or follow a business format and also the best practices and processes associated with it.

The franchiser company generally assists the independent owners significantly in launching and operating their businesses. In return, the business owners pay fees and royalties to franchiser. Hence, the franchisee acquires the right to use all the elements of a fully integrated business operation.

Some of the examples are fast-food restaurants such as McDonald's, Domino's Pizza, and KFC. Such franchisees maintain the design and styling aspects determined by the franchiser in their retail environments, ranging from the product offered to store design, ambience, atmospherics, and internal infrastructure to service standards to deliveries.

Product Franchises:

In these franchise agreements, the franchisee gets the right to use the brand/trade names, trademark, and/or products from the franchiser. Through this kind of agreement, manufacturers allow retailers to distribute their products and use their brand names and trademarks. They also monitor and control on the way retail stores distribute their products. In return of these rights, store owners pay royalties/fees or buy a minimum quantity of products.

Some of the examples are Tommy Hilfiger, Arrow, Scullers, Cotton King Stores, Reebok stores and Bata stores who operate under this kind of franchise agreement.

Manufacturing Franchises:

In this case, franchiser offers the right to produce and sell goods to a manufacturer under its brand name and trademark. This type of franchise is generally popular among food and beverage companies.

For example, soft drink bottlers and canners often obtain franchise rights from soft drink companies to produce, bottle, and distribute soft drinks. The major soft drink companies supply the concentrate to them, which are further processed, packed, and distributed by the regional manufacturing franchises.

One example is Gemini Distilleries Pvt. Ltd, Goa, a manufacturing franchise of Bacardi Ltd for manufacturing of winery products.

Business Opportunity Ventures:

This concept works on the format in which an independent business owner buys and distributes the products from one company. The company supplies the business owner with clients or accounts, in return of which the business owner pays the company a pre-decided fee.

For example, the business owners may obtain vending machine routes and distribution rights, through this type of franchise arrangement (e.g., coffee vending machine).

Retailer brands and companies often look toward franchising as a key operating model for expansion from scale, geographical coverage, and time perspectives.

Franchising is one of the modes of enterprise growth strategy.

- Entrepreneurs need this strategy when they need to expand their business beyond the area they are currently operating in.
- The franchise model is used as a method for increasing sales and brand visibility through independent business owners.

Franchising: Advantages and limitations to franchisor and franchisee

The franchisee is the third-party buyer who purchases the brand rights from the franchisor (the owner of the brand). The franchisee pays an initial franchise fee to the franchisor for the rights to use their brand in addition to ongoing franchise fees for marketing, royalties, and more.

There are several advantages of franchising for the franchisee, including:

Business assistance

One of the benefits of franchising for the franchisee is the business assistance they receive from the franchisor.

Depending on the terms of the franchise agreement and the structure of the business, the franchisee might receive essentially a turnkey business operation. They may be provided with the brand, the equipment, supplies, and the advertising plan—essentially everything they need to operate the business.

Other franchises may not provide everything, but all franchises provide the knowledge and wisdom of the franchisor. Whether that knowledge is stored in a searchable, digital knowledge base or is a phone number to reach the franchisor directly, the franchisee has access to a deep reservoir of business assistance to guide them through the process of owning and operating a business. This knowledge can be essential to running a successful business and makes it much easier than starting a business from scratch.

Brand recognition

A big benefit that franchisees receive when opening a franchise is brand recognition. If you start a business from scratch, you would have to build your brand and customer base from the ground up, which would take time.

Franchises, on the other hand, are already well-known businesses with established customer bases built in. So when you open a franchise with this recognizable branding, people will automatically know what your business is, what you provide, and what they can expect.

Lower failure rate
In general, franchises have a lower failure rate than solo businesses. When a franchisee buys into a franchise, they're joining a successful brand, as well as a network that will offer them support and advice, making it less likely they'll go out of business.

As well, franchises have already proven their business concept, so you have reassurance that the products or services you'll be offering are in demand.

Buying power
Another benefit of franchising is the sheer size of the network. If you're operating a standalone business and need to order products or supplies to make your products, you're paying more money per item because your order is relatively small.

However, a network of franchises has the opportunity to purchase goods at a deep discount by buying in bulk. The parent company can use the size of the network to negotiate deals that every franchisee benefits from. A lower cost of goods lowers the overall operation costs of the franchise.

Profits
In general, franchises see higher profits than independently established businesses. Most franchises have recognizable brands that bring customers in droves. This popularity results in higher profits. Even franchises that require a high initial investment for the franchise fee see high return on investment.

Lower risk
Starting a business is risky. This is true whether a business owner is opening an independent business or purchasing a franchise. That being said, the risk is lower when opening a franchise.

One of the reasons franchise owners face lower risk than independent business owners is the franchise network. Most franchises are owned by established corporations that have tested and proven the business model of the franchise in multiple markets.

Built-in customer base
One of the biggest struggles of any new business is finding customers. Franchises, on the other hand, come with instant brand recognition and a loyal customer base. Even if you're opening the first branch of a franchise in a small town, the likelihood is that potential customers are already familiar with the brand from exposure to TV commercials or travel to other cities.

Be your own boss
One of the biggest benefits of owning a business is being your own boss. When starting a franchise business, you get to be your own boss with the added benefit of receiving support from the franchise's knowledge base.

Owning a business is hard work, but when you're your own boss, you get to create your own schedule, have autonomy over your career, and potentially work from home.

Disadvantages of franchising for the franchisee
While there are many advantages of franchising, it would be remiss to think there aren't also disadvantages. Let us explain further.

Restricting regulations
While a franchise allows the franchisee to be their own boss, they're not entirely in control of their business, nor can they make decisions without taking into account the opinion of the franchisor.

For most franchisees, the most frustrating disadvantage that they face is that they must follow the restrictions laid out in the franchise agreement. The franchisor can exert a degree of control over the majority of the franchise business and decisions made by the franchisee.

These restrictions are put into place to maintain uniformity between the different franchises and the overall brand, but they can also be frustrating and feel limiting for the franchisee.

Initial cost
While the initial investment of the franchise fee buys a lot of benefits for the franchisee, it can also be costly —especially if you're joining a very well-known and profitable franchise. While this often translates to larger profits, coming up with this initial money can put a strain on any small business owner.

Even if you opt for a low-cost franchise, you'll likely still have to front a few thousand dollars. While this can be seen as a disadvantage of franchises, it's important to weigh the opportunity against the initial investment and find the right balance for your business. And keep in mind, there are also franchise financing options to help you come up with this initial cost.

Ongoing investment
In addition to the initial investment you'll have to provide to start your franchise, there are additional, ongoing costs that are unique to franchises. Within the franchise agreement, the ongoing costs of the franchise should be enumerated. These costs might include royalty fees, advertising costs, and a charge for training services.

Potential for conflict
While one of the benefits of owning a franchise is the network of support you receive, it also has the potential for conflict. Any close business relationship, especially when there's an imbalance of power, comes with a risk that the parties won't get along.

While a franchise agreement states the expectations of both the franchisee and franchisor, the franchisee has minimal power to enforce the franchise agreement without a costly legal battle. Whether it's lack of support or simply a clash of personalities, the closeness of the business relationship between franchisor and franchisee is rife for conflict. A franchisor should screen all potential franchisees before entering into business with them, and as the franchisor, you should also use this opportunity to get a feel for the franchisor's personality and management style.

Lack of financial privacy
Another disadvantage of franchising is a lack of privacy. The franchise agreement will likely stipulate that the franchisor can oversee the entire financial ecosystem of the franchise. This lack of financial privacy can be seen by franchisee as a disadvantage of owning a franchise; however, it may be less of an issue if you welcome financial guidance.

Advantages of franchising for the franchisor
The advantages and disadvantages of franchising don't solely apply to the franchisee, of course. The franchisor should also weigh the pros and cons before deciding to enter into this business model. First, let's explore the benefits of franchising that the franchisor can enjoy.

Access to capital
One of the biggest barriers to expansion for small business is the money it costs to expand. And while there are several business loan options, they don't always pan out. Franchising your business will take some time and money on your end, but it also has the potential to make you a lot of money in the form of franchise fees.

Expanding your business as a franchise allows you to expand with little debt. The business expands as capital becomes available from franchisees instead of taking on debt through loans. The franchisor also shares minimal risk with the franchisee because the franchisee puts their name on the deed for the physical location of the business and lowers the franchises overall liability.

Efficient growth
Opening the first unit of a business is costly and time consuming. Opening a second unit can be almost as difficult. When that burden is shared with another business owner, it makes the process more efficient and takes the onus off the initial business owner.

When trying to grow your small business, starting a franchise can make opening multiple locations a much simpler process.

Minimal employee supervision
One of the big stresses as a business owner is hiring and managing employees. As a franchisor, the only support that you have to provide to the franchisee is training and business knowledge. In general, the franchisor has no hand in the management, hiring, and firing of employees.

This minimal employee supervision allows the franchisor to focus on the growth of the business instead of day-to-day operations. Instead of worrying about whether an employee shows up for their shift or not, the franchisor is focused on the big picture for business success.

Increased brand awareness
One of the many benefits of franchising is increased brand awareness. The more locations the brand has, the more people who are aware of the brand. And the more these customers come to know and love the brand, the more profitable and successful the brand can be. This increased brand awareness of a multi-location franchise can be highly beneficial to the franchisor and their franchisees—a win-win.

Reduced risk
One of the biggest benefits to the franchisor in a franchise agreement is the ability to expand without an increase in risk. Because the franchisee takes on the debt and liability of opening a unit under the name of the franchise, the franchisor gets all the benefit of an additional location without taking on the risk themselves.
Additionally, the franchisor is often further insulated because the franchise is incorporated as a new business entity, leaving the original business owned by the franchisor as a separate entity from the franchise. A franchise lawyer can help to set up the terms for this type of protection within the franchise agreement.

Disadvantages of franchising for the franchisor
While franchisors receive a lot of benefits from starting a franchise, there are also some disadvantages to consider.

Loss of complete brand control
When a business owner opens an independent business, they maintain complete control over their brand and every decision that happens within the business.

When a franchisor allows a franchisee to open a business under their brand, they're giving away (actually, selling) some of the control over their small business branding. While the franchise agreement should contain strong stipulations and rules to guide the decisions made by the franchisee, your franchisees won't be clones of you. They will think and act differently, and your brand could wind up suffering because of it.

Increased potential for legal disputes
Any time you enter into a close business agreement with other people, you open yourself to the risk of legal disputes. While a well-crafted and lawyer-approved franchise agreement should limit a lot of the possibilities for legal disputes between the franchisor and franchisees, these disputes are still possible.

Any legal disputes that must be resolved in mediation or through the court system can be costly in both time and money, which takes away from the success of the franchise.

Initial investment
While much conversation is devoted to the initial investment that a franchisee must make in the franchise, that ignores the initial cost that is taken on by the franchisor.

When a franchisor starts a franchise, there's a startup cost to get the business in operation. A franchisor must make sure that the franchise agreement is written clearly and reviewed by a lawyer experienced in franchise law. You may also hire a franchise consultant for expertise during this process. Starting a franchise requires an initial investment of both time and money on the part of the franchisor.

Federal and state regulation
While not entirely a drawback, dealing with the federal regulations set down by the Federal Trade Commission for franchises can be a nuisance for franchisors. These regulations ensure that franchises are operated fairly, but it also requires time and effort from the franchisors to meet all of these regulations.

And while you don't have to file your agreement with the federal government, you do have to file with some states—and you will have to make sure you're compliant with different state's laws. This can be a time-consuming process, but can be made easier with professional guidance.

There are two ways of growing a business i.e., internal expansion and external expansion.

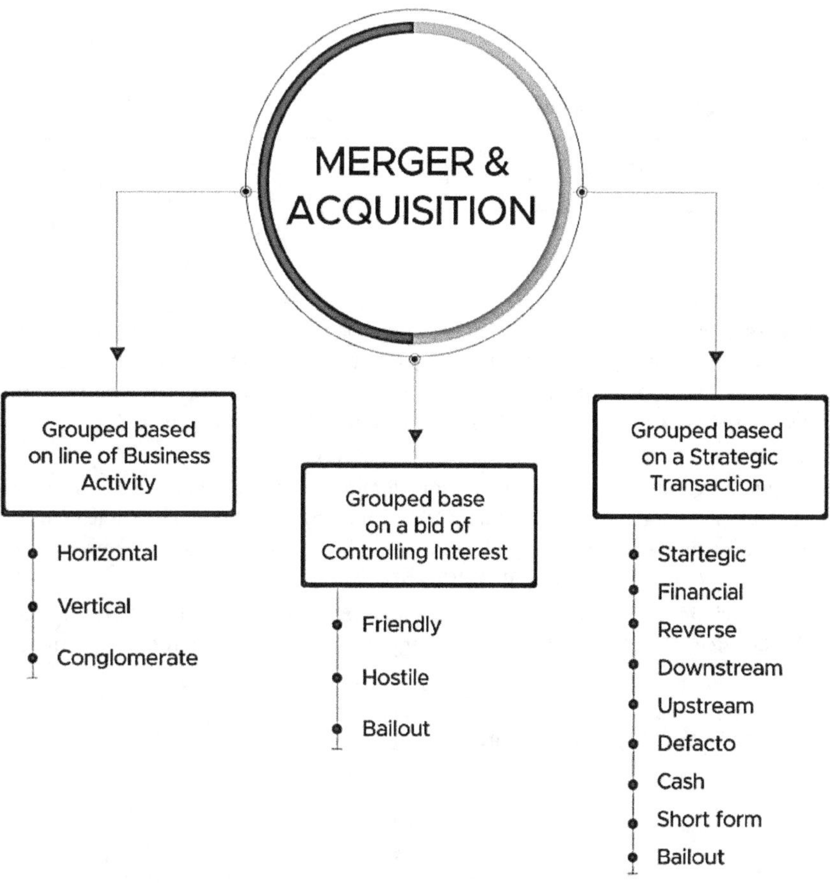

An entrepreneur may grow its business in either of these two ways

- **Internal Expansion:** A firm grows gradually over time in the normal course of the business, through the acquisition of new assets, replacement of technologically obsolete equipment, and the establishment of new lines of products.
- **External Expansion:** A firm acquires a running business and grows overnight through corporate combinations. These combinations are in the form of mergers, acquisitions, amalgamations, and takeovers and have now become important features of corporate restructuring. The external expansion has been playing an important role in the external growth of a number of leading companies the world over. They have become popular because of the enhanced competition, breaking of trade barriers, free flow of capital across countries, and globalization of businesses.
- From the above, we can see that mergers and acquisitions (M&A) are a common form of the external expansion strategy. Now, we will study the concept and other related aspects of M&A.

Mergers

A merger is a combination of two or more businesses into one business.

- In other words, the merging of two companies where one new company will continue to exist is known as a merger.
- For example, Company A and Company B merge to form a new Company C. Company A and Company B will cease to exist and Company C will be formed. The merger is also known as amalgamation.

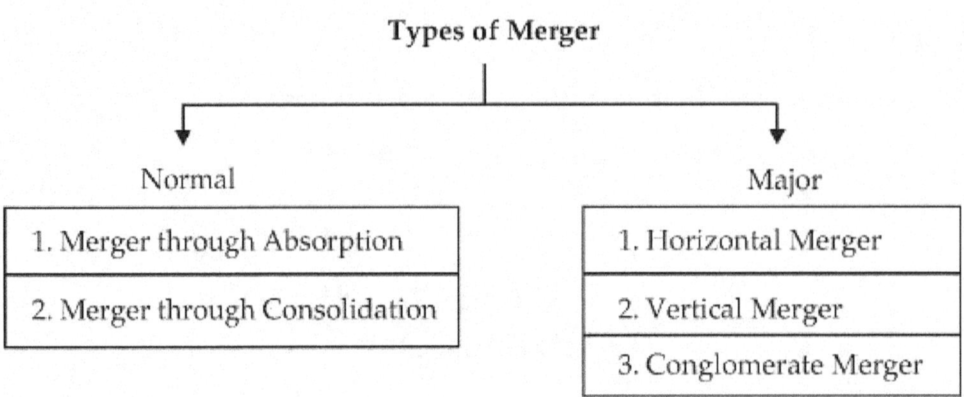

There are two types of merger

- **Merger through Absorption:** Absorption is a combination of two or more companies into an 'existing company'. All companies except one lose their identity in such a merger. For example, absorption of Tata Fertilizers Ftd., (TFF) by Tata Chemicals Ftd., (TCL). TCF, an acquiring company (a buyer), survived after merger while TFF, an acquired company (a seller), ceased to exist. TFF transferred its assets, liabilities and shares to TCF.

- **Merger through Consolidation:** A consolidation is a combination of two or more companies into a 'new company. In this form of merger, all companies are legally dissolved and a new entity is created. Here, the acquired company transfers its assets, liabilities, and shares to the acquiring company for cash or exchange of shares. For example, the merger of Hindustan Computers Ltd, Hindustan Instruments Ltd, Indian Software Company Ltd, and Indian Reprographics Ltd into an entirely new company called HCL Ltd.

- A fundamental characteristic of merger (either through absorption or consolidation) is that the acquiring company (existing or new) takes over the ownership of other companies and combines their operations with its own operations.

Besides, there are three major types of mergers

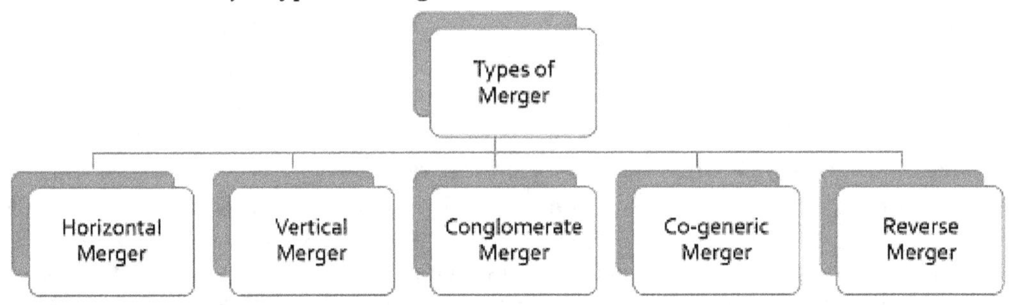

- **Horizontal Merger:** Two firms are merged across similar products or services. Horizontal mergers are often used as a way for a company to increase its market share by merging with a competing company. For example, combining of two book publishers or two luggage manufacturing companies to gain dominant market share.

- **Vertical Merger:** Two firms are merged along the value-chain, such as a manufacturer merging with a supplier. Vertical mergers are often used as a way to gain a competitive advantage within the marketplace. For example, joining of a TV manufacturing(assembling) company and a TV marketing company or joining of a spinning company and a weaving company. The vertical merger may take the form of forward or backward merger. When a company combines with the supplier of material, it is called backward merger and when it combines with the customer, it is known as forward merger.

- **Conglomerate Merger:** Two firms in completely different industries merge, such as a gas pipeline company merging with a high technology company. Conglomerates are usually used as a way to smooth out wide fluctuations in earnings and provide more consistency in long-term growth. For example, merging of different businesses like manufacturing of cement products, fertilizer products, electronic products, insurance investment, and advertising agencies. L&T and Voltas Ltd are examples of such mergers.

Acquisitions

Acquisition is another form of external expansion strategy available to an entrepreneur.

- An acquisition may be defined as an act of acquiring effective control by one company over assets or management of another company without any combination of companies.

- In other words, in an acquisition, two or more companies may remain independent, separate legal entities, but there may be a change in control of the companies. When an acquisition is 'forced' or 'unwilling', it is called a takeover.
- In an unwilling acquisition, the management of 'target' company would oppose a move of being taken over. But, when managements of acquiring and target companies mutually and willingly agree to the takeover, it is called an acquisition or friendly takeover.

Advantages of Mergers & Acquisitions

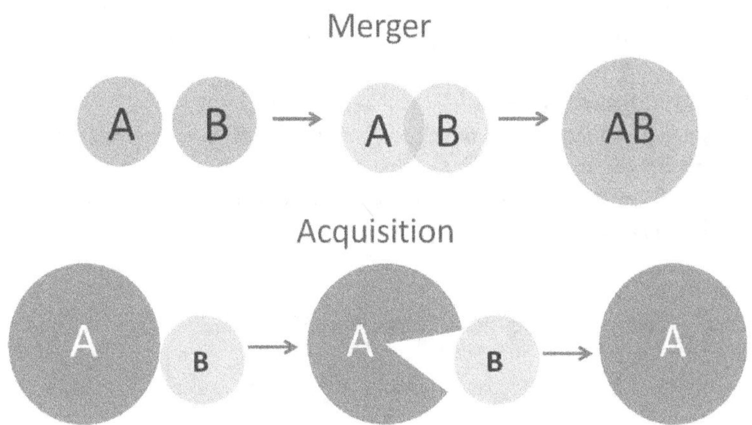

The following are the advantages of Mergers & Acquisition:

- **Achieving Business Growth:** M&A helps in achieving business growth in a situation when its internal growth is constrained due to a paucity of resources. Internal growth requires that a company should develop its operating facilities- manufacturing, research, marketing, etc. But, lack or inadequacy of resources and time needed for internal development may constrain a company's pace of growth. Hence, a company can acquire production facilities as well as other resources from outside through M&A. Also, for entering new products/markets, the company may lack technical skills and may require special marketing skills and a wide distribution network to access different segments of markets. The company can acquire an existing company or companies with the requisite infrastructure and skills and grow quickly.
- **Economies of Scale:** It arises when large-scale production leads to a reduction in per unit cost of production. This is because, with merger, fixed costs like rent, administration costs, etc. are distributed over a large volume of production causing the unit cost of production to decline. Economies of scale may also arise from other indivisibilities such as production facilities, management functions, and management resources and systems. This is because a given function, facility or resource is utilized for a large scale of operations by the combined firm.
- **Operating Synergy:** It indicates a situation where the combined firm is more valuable than the sum of the individual combining firms. It refers to benefits other than those related to economies of scale. Operating economies are one form of synergy benefits.
- **Managerial Synergy:** Apart from operating economies, synergy may also arise from enhanced managerial capabilities, creativity, innovativeness, R&D and market coverage capacity due to the complementarity of resources and skills and a widened horizon of opportunities.
- **Financial Synergy:** A merger may result in financial synergy and benefits for the firm in many ways like the elimination of financial constraints, enhancement of debt capacity, and lowering the financial costs in the form of lower interest.

Procedure for Evaluating the Decision for Mergers and Acquisitions

An entrepreneur should analyze three important steps for evaluating mergers and acquisitions are:

- **Planning:** It includes analysis of industry-specific and firm-specific information. An entrepreneur should review its objective of acquisition in the context of its strengths and weaknesses and corporate goals. For this purpose, industry data will be required on market growth, nature of competition, ease of entry, capital and labor intensity, degree of regulation, etc. This data will help in indicating the product-market strategies that are appropriate for the company. It will also help the firm in identifying the business units that should be dropped or added. On the other hand, the target firm (which is going to be acquired) will need information about the quality of management, market share, and size, capital structure, profitability, production and marketing capabilities, etc. of the entrepreneur's firm.
- **Search and Screening:** Search focuses on how and where to look for suitable candidates for acquisition. The screening process short-lists a few candidates from many available and obtains detailed information about each of them.

- **Financial Evaluation:** Financial evaluation of a merger is needed to determine the earnings and cash flows, areas of risk, the maximum price payable to the target company, and the best way to finance the merger. In a competitive market situation, the current market value is the correct and fair value of the share of the target firm. The target firm will not accept any offer below the current market value of its share.

- The target firm may, in fact, expect the offer price to be more than the current market value of its share since it may expect that merger benefits will accrue to the acquiring firm.

- From the above discussion, it can be inferred that the decision pertaining to merger and acquisition involves careful analysis of various factors before taking the final decision. An entrepreneur should look at all these factors and decide in favour of it if it works in the direction in which the firm should grow and expand.

Franchising: Advantages and limitations

Franchising is a business arrangement in which the franchisor grants the franchisee the right to operate a business using its established brand, systems, and support in exchange for fees and ongoing royalties. Franchising offers both advantages and limitations for both the franchisor (the company granting the franchise) and the franchisee (the individual or company operating the franchise). Let's explore these in more detail:

Advantages for the Franchisor

- **Expansion of the brand:** Franchising allows the franchisor to expand its brand presence rapidly and reach new markets without substantial capital investment.
- **Revenue generation:** Franchise fees, ongoing royalties, and other revenue streams from franchisees provide a consistent source of income for the franchisor.
- **Reduced operational costs:** Franchisees are responsible for setting up and operating their individual franchises, resulting in reduced operational costs for the franchisor.
- **Shared risks:** Franchisees bear the risks associated with individual franchise operations, reducing the financial risks for the franchisor.

Limitations for the Franchisor

- **Loss of control:** Franchising involves sharing control over the business with franchisees, which can result in less direct control over operations and potential variations in quality.
- **Reputation risk:** If franchisees do not adhere to the brand standards or provide poor customer experiences, it can negatively impact the overall reputation of the franchisor.
- **Legal and support obligations:** Franchisors have legal and support obligations to provide training, ongoing support, and monitoring to franchisees, which can require additional resources and effort.

Advantages for the Franchisee

- **Established brand and systems:** Franchisees benefit from using an established brand, proven business systems, and operational support, which can increase their chances of success.
- **Reduced risk:** Franchisees enter into a business model that has already been tested and proven successful, reducing the risk associated with starting a new business from scratch.
- **Training and support:** Franchisors often provide comprehensive training, ongoing support, and access to marketing and advertising resources, helping franchisees operate their business effectively.
- **Economies of scale:** Franchisees can leverage the purchasing power of the franchisor and benefit from economies of scale in sourcing supplies and materials.

Limitations for the Franchisee

- **High upfront costs:** Franchisees typically need to pay an initial franchise fee and invest in the setup and initial operating costs, which can be substantial.
- **Ongoing fees:** Franchisees are required to pay ongoing royalties and possibly additional fees to the franchisor, which can impact their profitability.
- **Lack of flexibility:** Franchisees must adhere to the franchisor's established systems, guidelines, and brand standards, limiting their ability to make independent business decisions.
- **Dependency on the franchisor:** Franchisees rely on the franchisor for support, marketing, and the overall success of the brand. If the franchisor faces difficulties or makes poor decisions, it can impact the franchisee's business.

It's important to note that the advantages and limitations of franchising can vary depending on the specific franchise system and the terms of the franchise agreement. It is advisable for both franchisors and franchisees to thoroughly evaluate the opportunities and risks involved before entering into a franchise arrangement.

1. The strategy was developed by the visionary chief executive in which mode of strategic management?
   A. Planning mode
   B. Strategic mode
   C. Adaptive mode
   D. Entrepreneurial mode

Answer: D

Explanation:

Strategies are developed by visionary managers in strategically managed entrepreneurial mode.

2. What type of strategy is stability strategy?
   A. Corporate level
   B. Functional level
   C. Strategic level
   D. Business level

Answer: A

Explanation:

Corporate level strategy is stability strategy.

3. What type of range is the impact of strategies on the general direction and basic character of a company?
   A. Medium range
   B. Short range
   C. Long-rangenge
   D. Minimal

Answer: C

Explanation:

Long-rangenge is the impact of strategies on the general direction and basic character of a company.

4. Select the statement which is much more accurate:
   A. Means value for money
   B. Is described as the benefits chosen by the business to give customers through their product/service
   C. Is the benefits of a product/service which is perceived by the customers
   D. Does not offer a competitive advantage

Answer: C

Explanation:

Value is the perceived profitability of the product/service by the customer. The value proposition is a comparison of the benefits offered by a company's products and services with the price paid to its customers.

5. Which statement best applies to emergent strategies:
   A. Implies an ability to react to the events
   B. Implies strategizing
   C. Implies no deviation from plans
   D. Implies constant evaluation of the bigger picture

Answer: A

Explanation:

Implies an ability to react to the events best applies to emergent strategies.

6. Which of the following shows concern for non-profit organizations?
   A. The markets to service
   B. Identifying suppliers to deal with
   C. Developing capabilities
   D. Building monopolies

Answer: A

Explanation:

The markets for the following services are related to non-profits.

7. The strategic management process is:
   A. Set of activities that are guaranteed to prevent organizational failure
   B. A process that is concerned with a firm's resources, capabilities, and competencies, but not the conditions in its external environment
   C. A set of activities which has not been used successfully in the not-for-profit sector
   D. A dynamic process involving the full set of commitments, decisions, and actions related to the firm

Answer: D

Explanation:

The strategic management process is A dynamic process involving the full set of commitments, decisions, and actions related to the firm.

8. Organizations require good people with appropriate skills and abilities to work together effectively to be successful. Which are the characteristics is not seen as critical for this?
   - **A.** Competent
   - **B.** Committed
   - **C.** Cost-effective
   - **D.** Capable

Answer: D

Explanation:

Capable characteristics is not seen as critical for this. Strategic management makes employees capable of understanding the market reactions to organization's product and taking corrective measures for the organization.

9. State the assumptions of Hard human resource management?
   - **A.** Employees tend to be more productive when they are better informed
   - **B.** Employees tend to be more productive when they are committed to the organization
   - **C.** Employees are that resources can be used effectively in the search for competitive advantage
   - **D.** Employees have to be trusted to make correct decisions

Answer: C

Explanation:

Hard Human Management assumes that it is a resource that employees must effectively use to pursue their competitive advantage.

10. Which of the following is the characteristic of human resource management?
   - **A.** Managers are responsible for the employees
   - **B.** Teams tend to provide increased productivity
   - **C.** Managers are responsible for deploying employees
   - **D.** For dealing with employees, scientific management principles and systems

Answer: B

Explanation:

The team ensures that productivity gains are characteristic of mild human resource management. Soft Human Resources Management (HRM) is an approach to human resource management that treats employees as one of the company's most important assets.

11. A possible and desirable future state of an organisation is called:
   - **A.** Mission
   - **B.** Strategy implementation
   - **C.** Strategy formulation
   - **D.** Vision

Answer: D

Explanation:

The possible desirable future state of the organization is called the vision.

12. The question mark in the BCG matrix symbolizes:
   - **A.** Invest
   - **B.** Stable
   - **C.** Liquidate
   - **D.** Remain diversified

Answer: D

Explanation:

The question mark in the BCG matrix symbolizes Remain diversified.

13. Selling all of a company's assets in parts of their tangible worth is called:
   - **A.** Divestiture
   - **B.** Liquidation
   - **C.** Concentric diversification
   - **D.** Unrelated integration

Answer: C

Explanation:

Selling all of a company's assets in parts of their tangible worth is called Concentric diversification.

14. Cash cows in the BCG matrix symbolize:
   - **A.** Invest
   - **B.** Stable
   - **C.** Liquidate
   - **D.** Remain diversified

Answer: C

Explanation:

Cash cows in the BCG matrix symbolize Liquidate.

15. BCG matrix is based on:

    A. Attractiveness of industry and business strength   **B.** Growth of industry and business strength

    C. Attractiveness of industry and relative market share   **D.** Growth rate of industry and relative market share

Answer: D

Explanation:

The BCG Matrix is based on industry growth and relative market share. The BCG Matrix is a framework developed by the Boston Consulting Group that assesses the strategic position and potential of a corporate brand portfolio.

16. State the guides to decision making:

    A. Rules   **B.** Procedures

    C. Goals   **D.** Policies

Answer: D

Explanation:

Policies are decision-making guidelines. A policy is a permanent plan that provides decision-making guidelines.

17. How long is the long term in strategic thinking approximately?

    A. 1 month to 1 year   **B.** 2 to 3 years

    C. 3 to 5 years   **D.** More than 5 years

Answer: D

Explanation:

In strategic thinking, more than five years is long-term. Most strategic plans look ahead about three to 5 years.

18. One company buying another company means:

    A. Joint venture   **B.** Acquisition

    C. Amalgamation   **D.** Merger

Answer: B

Explanation:

When a company buys another company, it means an acquisition. An acquisition is the purchase of most or all of the shares of one company in order to gain control of another.

19. Low cost, focus and differentiation are examples of:

    A. Corporate strategies   **B.** Operational strategies

    C. Business strategies   **D.** Functional strategies

Answer: C

Explanation:

Low cost, differentiation and concentration are examples of business strategies. Low-priced sellers strive to sell their products at the lowest possible prices while making a profit so that they can attract customers to the market.

20. How many cells are there in a SWOT matrix?

    A. 9   **B.** 6

    C. 3   **D.** 2

Answer: A

Explanation:

SWOT Matrix contains 9 cells in which four are key factor cells, four strategy cells and one blank cell.

Chapter - 5 Business Arithmetic

Introduction

Business Mathematics consists of Mathematical concepts related to business. It comprises mainly profit, loss and interest. Maths is the base of any business. Business Mathematics financial formulas, measurements which helps to calculate profit and loss, the interest rates, tax calculations, salary calculations, which helps to finish the business tasks effectively and efficiently.

Importance of Business Arithmetic

Business Arithmetic will help the entrepreneur to do a careful analysis of various options available to him or her for business strategy.

- In the previous chapters, we studied various topics like a business plan, growth strategy, marketing, etc.
- All these analysis require some mathematical tools and formulae to be used.
- In this chapter, some of the concepts to understand their application are discussed.

Cost-Volume-Profit Analysis (CVP) Analysis

Managerial accounting methods provide techniques for evaluating the viability and ability to grow or "scale" a business. These techniques are called cost-volume-profit analysis (CVP).

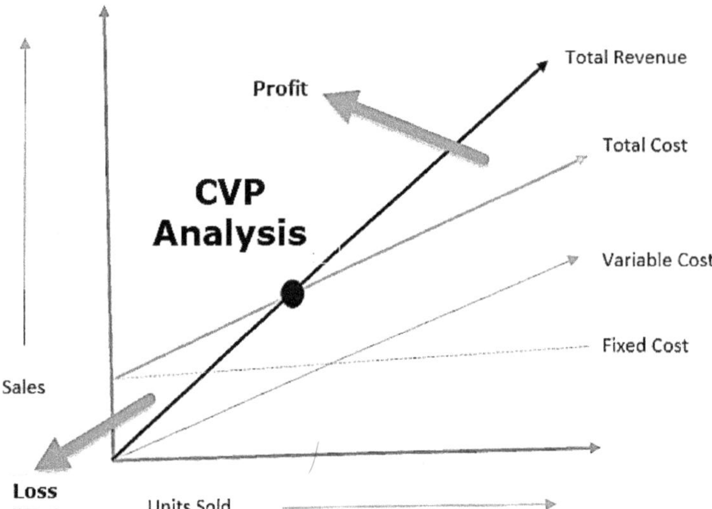

- An entrepreneur should be aware of certain concepts of cost and revenue to analyze the number of products to be produced to ensure that the desirable profitability is achieved.
- This is part of managerial accounting which helps in taking effective decisions.
- CVP means developing an understanding of the nature and behavior of an entity's costs.
- In order to understand how a business is going to perform over time and with shifts in volume, it is imperative to first consider the cost structure of the business.
- This requires a detailed study of specific types of costs that are to be incurred and trying to understand their unique characteristics. Break-even analysis is one of the tools of CVP analysis.

Unit of Sale: It is defined as the measure of what products are sold.
Unit cost: Cost of unit can be defined as the cost incurred by a company to produce, store and sell one unit of sale of a particular product or service.

Break-Even Analysis

In today's complex business world, bringing a balance amongst variables like revenue, cost, profit, etc. is a tedious task. Managerial economists use various tools to analyze these variables.

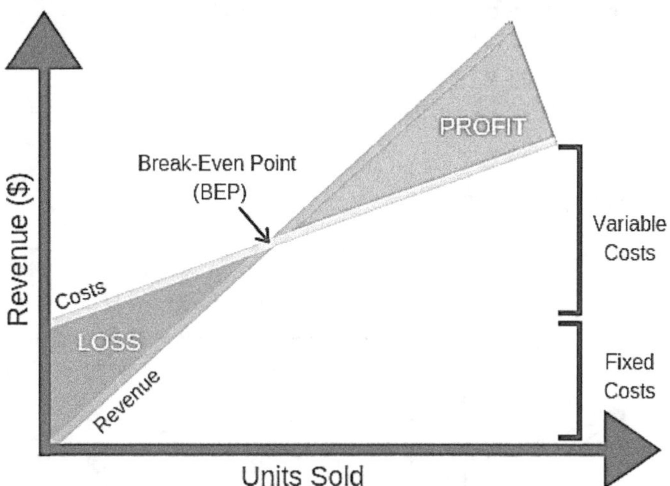

- Break-Even Analysis is one of the most efficient tools to analyze revenue, cost, and profit variables and bring a balance between them.
- Break-Even Analysis seeks to analyze Break-Even Point (BEP) which is the point of equality between sales and cost. In other words, **BEP indicates no profit no loss situation** for a firm.
- The importance of the break-even point lies in the fact that it sets up bottom-line sales for managers below which the firm would be incurring losses. It is an efficient technique of managing sales and costs.
- **Break-even analysis** may be defined as the analysis of cost elements like fixed cost and variable cost and their impact on a firm's sales and profits. It is also termed as cost volume profit (CVP) analysis.
- Under break-even point analysis, the total cost is segregated between fixed and variable costs.
- **Fixed Cost** It is the cost element that is not affected by changes in the level of production like Rent, Salary of employees, etc.
- **Variable Cost**: It is the cost element that changes with the change in the level of production like raw material, labour, etc.

The margin of safety in value (₹) = Actual Sales (₹) - BES (₹))
Margin of safety in units = Actual Sales (units) - BES (units)

- The margin of safety indicates an excess of actual sales over break-even sales.
- It helps managers to analyze how safe the business is positioned from incurring losses.
- A higher margin of safety indicates a strong business position in terms of sales and cost. On the other hand, a lower margin of safety indicates a weak business position in terms of cost and sales.

Importance or Use of Cash Flow Projections
Cash flow projection indicates the cash inflow and outflow estimates for a particular period.

- An entrepreneur should always have visibility for the cash position of the business venture. It enables a better working capital planning of the business.
- If a business runs out of cash and is not able to obtain new finance, it will become insolvent. It is no excuse for management to claim that they didn't see a cash flow crisis coming.
- So, in business, "cash is king". Cash flow is the life-blood of all businesses - particularly start-ups and small enterprises.
- As a result, it is essential that management forecast (predict) what is going to happen to cash flow to make sure the business has enough to survive.

The following are the importance of cash flow projection
- Cash flow projection helps in identifying potential shortfalls in cash balances in advance. It acts as an "early warning system". This is a very important reason to have a cash flow projection.
- It ensures that the entrepreneur can afford to pay suppliers and employees. Suppliers who don't get paid will soon stop supplying the business; it is even worse if employees are not paid on time.

- It helps to spot problems with customer payments. It also encourages the business to look at how quickly customers are paying their debts.
- External stakeholders such as banks may require a regular forecast. Certainly if the business has a bank loan, the bank will want to look at cash flow forecasts at regular intervals.

Budgeting and Managing the Finances

Another important exercise for an entrepreneur is to prepare a budget for future years and managing the company finances accordingly.

The process of preparing budgets is as follows

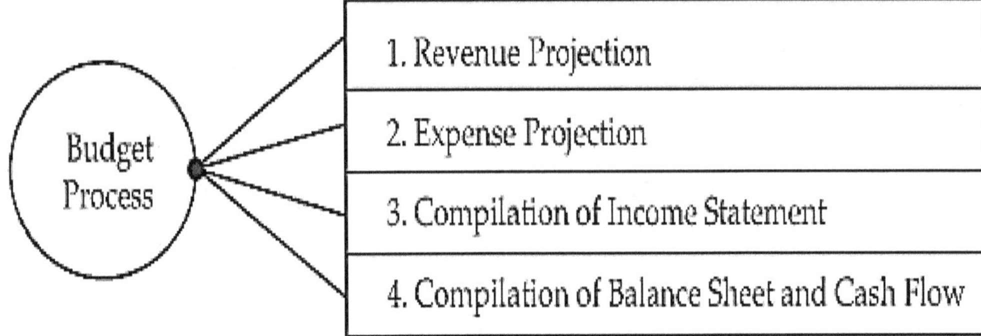

- **Revenue Projection:** Revenue projection will be based on the projected quantity to be sold and the price of the product in the next years. The estimated revenue is derived by multiplying the quantity sold with a price.
- **Expense Projection:** Expense estimate will be based on the future operational plan of the business and the resources required for the period. Each department should estimate its expense and get it approved before it is compiled in the final budget.
- **Compilation of Income Statement:** Once a future estimate of the revenue and expense is finalized then it is compiled in the income statement to show the estimated profitability of the business. Profitability will be determined by deducting expenses from the revenue.
- **Compilation of Balance Sheet and Cash Flow:** The balance sheet is prepared on the basis of capital expenditure projected for the future years and debtors and creditors projection. Similarly, a cash flow statement is prepared for estimating the cash requirements.

Computation of Working Capital

Working capital is the difference between current assets and current liabilities. It measures the liquidity or cash availability for day-to-day business operations.

- Current assets refer to cash or the assets which can be converted into cash in the next 12 months like debtors, bills receivable, short-term investment, inventory, prepaid expense, etc.
- Similarly, current liabilities refer to the obligations for payment to vendors or other parties in the next 12 months like creditors, bills payable.

Inventory Control and Economic Order Quantity (EOQ)

Inventory control is an important aspect of the production planning process. The key decision to inventory control is how much stock one should hold to bring a balance between the demand and investment cost in such stock levels. In other words, inventory control is concerned with minimizing the total cost of inventory. There are three factors that affect the inventory control decision:

- **The cost of holding the stock:** The interest cost of the money invested in holding stock.
- **The cost of placing an order:** This involves postage cost, tendering cost etc.
- **The cost of shortage:** looking for alternative arrangements if there is shortage of stock in the factory.

There are different levels of stock that can be maintained depending on the size of the business and the level of demand of the product in the market. Broadly there are three levels of inventory.

Reorder Level

The reorder level is the inventory level at which an entity should issue a purchase order to replenish the quantity on hand. When calculated correctly, the reorder level should result in replenishment inventory arriving just as the existing inventory quantity has declined to zero.

The formula for reorder level is Maximum Consumption x Maximum Reorder Period For example, maximum consumption 1,000 units per week, Delivery time 8-10 weeks.

Reorder level = 1,000 x 10 = 10,000 units.

Minimum Level

- The minimum level of inventory is that level that is needful for continuing of production without any disturbance.
- With simple mathematical formula, we can calculate this level. Always this stock should be in the store or factory.
- When the inventory will go to the minimum level, the production or store department should send the notice of inventory requirement to the purchase department.
- Minimum Level = Reorder Level - (Normal Consumption x Normal Reorder Period)
- For example, maximum consumption 1,000 units per week, normal consumption 750 units per week, minimum consumption 500 units per week. Delivery time 8-10 weeks. Reorder level 10,000 units.
- Minimum Level = 10,000 - (750 x 9) = 3250 Units
- We have a minimum level of 3,250 units which means, when there are only 3,250 units in our stock, we should issue the purchase order or manage for getting stock at the earliest, otherwise production will stop and our machine and labor and other invested capital will be free.
- So, our fixed cost will increase.

Maximum Level

- The maximum level of inventory is the maximum quantity of material which have to keep in store.
- We should not keep the stock more than the maximum level because if we keep more stock than the maximum level it will increase the cost of capital because we do not need the stock more than maximum level.
- Excess stock than maximum level will increase the cost of storing.
- Maximum Level = Reorder Level + Economic Order Quantity - (Minimum rate of usage x Minimum lead time)
- For example, maximum consumption 1,000 units per week, normal consumption 750 units per week, minimum consumption 500 units per week.
- Delivery time 8-10 weeks. Reorder level 10,000 units, Economic Order Quantity 7,500 Units.
- Maximum Level = 10,000 + 7,500 - (500 x 8) 13,500 Units

Economic Order Quantity

Economic Order Quantity (EOQ) is a simple inventory management model to determine the point at which the combination of inventory order costs and inventory carrying costs are the least. In other words, EOQ represents the balance between the inventory ordering cost and inventory carrying cost. It indicates the most cost-effective quantity to order. EOQ is beneficial when you have repetitive purchasing of an item.

The formula for EOQ is as Follows

The total cost of inventory is the sum of the purchase, ordering and holding costs. As a formula: **TC = PC + OC + HC**, where TC is the Total Cost; PC is Purchase Cost; OC is Ordering Cost; and HC is Holding Cost.

- **Annual Usage:** This is expressed in units and based on prior-year unit sales or forecasted unit sales or a combination of both.
- **Order Cost:** This is the sum of the costs that are incurred each time an item is ordered. These costs are associated with:
  (i) Physical activities are required to process the order as well as the costs charged to ship and receive the stock.
  (ii) Cost to enter the purchase order, cost to communicate with the vendor, the cost to process the receipt, incoming inspection, invoice processing and vendor payment, inbound freight, and insurance associated with the shipment.
- **Carrying Cost:** Carrying costs are the variable costs per unit of holding an item in inventory. Below are the primary components of carrying cost.
  (a) Interest: If an inventory is built upon the basis of borrowed money then the interest accumulated on that borrowed money will form part of the carrying cost.
  (b) Insurance: Insurance costs are directly related to the total value of the inventory. Hence, it should be included as part of the carrying cost.

(c) Storage Costs: Storage costs should only include costs that are variable based upon inventory levels.

This means that if the sales do not fluctuate then one should order 400 units every quarter to keep the ordering and carrying cost at a minimum level.

Return on Investment (ROI) and return one quity (ROE)

Investors and financial professionals use a wide variety of tools to measure their profits and success. Return on equity and return on investment are two common tools that provide insight into a company's financial health. If you're interested in investing or a career in finance, learning how to use each of these may prepare you for success.

Return on equity (ROE)
Return on equity is a ratio you can use to measure the financial performance of a company based on its shareholders' equity. ROE may help business executives focus on the management and decision-making processes in the financial aspects of their work. Rather than factoring in the company's debt, ROE determines how effectively the business uses its assets to make a profit. Investors often use ROE to determine whether a company can grow and use investments effectively. Because of this, companies often strive for an ROE that's above the average for their industry. When investors compare a company to one of its competitors, the one with the higher ROE may have a higher possibility of receiving the investor's financial support.

Return on investment (ROI)
Return on investment is a ratio you can use to measure the financial return that a company receives from an investment. This provides business executives with an understanding of the company's financial standing. ROI focuses on the profitability of an investment to help investors determine whether to commit funds to it. This ratio factors in debt to provide a comprehensive overview of the company's investments.

ROI is a versatile metric that you may use for many purposes, such as evaluating a stock investment or marketing campaign. While it's often best to have a high ROI, this calculation may not consider the risk of a particular investment. Using ROI with other financial metrics, such as risk analysis, can provide more helpful insights.

- Return on investment and return on equity are two important measures of the profitability performance of the firm.
- An entrepreneur should calculate and analyze these two ratios to assess the profitability of the business.
- Return on Investment (ROI) is a performance measure used to evaluate the efficiency of an investment or to compare the efficiency of a number of different investments.
- Return on Equity (ROE) is the amount of net income returned as a percentage of shareholder's equity.
- Return on equity measures a corporation's profitability by revealing how much profit a company generates with the money shareholders have invested.

Multiple Choice Questions

1. ABC Company produces and sells a product with a selling price of $50 per unit. The variable cost per unit is $30, and the total fixed costs are $80,000.
   What is the financial breakeven point for ABC Company in terms of the number of units it needs to sell?

   A. 2,000 units   **B.** 3000 units

   C. 4000 units   **D.** 5000 units

Answer: C

Explanation:

To calculate the financial breakeven point, we need to determine the number of units ABC Company needs to sell in order to cover its total fixed costs. The contribution margin per unit can be calculated by subtracting the variable cost per unit from the selling price per unit:

Contribution margin per unit = Selling price per unit - Variable cost per unit

Contribution margin per unit = $50 - $30 = $20

Next, we can use the contribution margin per unit to find the number of units needed to cover the fixed costs:

Breakeven point (in units) = Total fixed costs / Contribution margin per unit

Breakeven point (in units) = $80,000 / $20 = 4,000 units

Therefore, the financial breakeven point for ABC Company is 4,000 units.

2. Breakeven point is the point where:

   A. fixed and variable cost lines intersect   **B.** fixed and total cost lines intersect

   C. variable and total cost lines intersect   **D.** sales revenue and total cost lines intersect

Answer: D

Explanation:
Breakeven point is the point where sales revenue and total cost lines intersect.

3. Break-even point is not affected with the changes in which one of the following?
   A. Sale price per unit
   B. Variable cost per unit
   C. Number of units sold
   D. Total fixed costs

Answer: C

Explanation:
Break-even point is not affected with the changes in Number of units sold.

4. In the context of operating leverage break-even analysis, if selling price per unit rises and all other variables remain constant, the operating break-even point in units will:
   A. Fall
   B. Rise
   C. Stay the same
   D. Still be indeterminate until interest and preferred dividends paid are known

Answer: A

Explanation:
In the context of operating leverage break-even analysis, if selling price per unit rises and all other variables remain constant, the operating break-even point in units will Fall.

5. At break even point slope of sales line is equal to:
   A. $\dfrac{\text{Variable Expenses + Constant Expenses}}{\text{Total Sales}}$
   B. $\dfrac{\text{Total Sales}}{\text{Total Expenses}}$
   C. $\dfrac{\text{Total Sales} - \text{Profit}}{\text{Variable Expenses + Profit}}$
   D. $\dfrac{\text{Variable Expenses} - \text{Constant Expenses}}{\text{Total Sales}}$

Answer: A

Explanation:
At break even point slope of sales line is equal to $\dfrac{\text{Variable Expenses + Constant Expenses}}{\text{Total Sales}}$.

6. Break-even analysis chart is drawn between:
   A. overhead cost and fixed cost
   B. volume of production and income
   C. material cost and labour cost
   D. none of these

Answer: B

Explanation:
Break-even analysis chart is drawn between volume of production and income.

7. The difference between actual sales and breakeven point is known as:
   A. Margin of safety
   B. Price-cost margin
   C. Contribution
   D. Profit

Answer: A

Explanation:
The Margin of safety is the difference between the break-even point and output is produced.

8. Fixed cost of an equipment is Rs. 6,000, if variable cost of an item it produces is Rs. 2 per item and sells it for Rs. 7 per item, what is the break-even point?
   A. 1200 items
   B. 3000 items
   C. 7000 items
   D. 6500 items

Answer: A

Explanation:

$$\text{Break even point} = \frac{\text{Total fixed cost } (TFC)}{\text{Price per unit } (P) - \text{Variable cost } (V.C)}$$

Given:

TFC $=$ Rs. 6000

P $=$ Rs. 7

VC $=$ Rs. 2 per item

Break even point $= \dfrac{6000}{7-2} = 1200$

∴ Break-even point $= 1200$ items

9. The data for break-even analysis of a product are given as-fixed cost is Rs. 10,000; variable cost is Rs. 10/unit; selling price is Rs. 15/unit. The break-even volume is:

A. 2000
B. 2500
C. 3500
D. 4000

Answer: A

Explanation:

BEP in terms of physical unit:

$$BEP = X_{BEP} = \frac{\text{Total Fixed cost}}{\text{Contribution per unit}} = \frac{F}{s-v}$$

where F is the fixed cost
s = sales price of one product, v = variable cost of one product

Given:
$F = $ Rs. $10000, s = $ Rs. 15 and $v = $ Rs. 10

$$\text{Break-Even Quantity} = \frac{F}{s-v}$$

$$\therefore BEP = \frac{F}{s-v} = \frac{10000}{15-10} = 2000 \text{ units.}$$

10. Break-even point is not affected with the changes in which one of the following?

A. Sale price per unit
B. Variable cost per unit
C. Number of units sold
D. Total fixed costs

Answer: C

Explanation:
Break-even point is not affected with the changes in Number of units sold.

11. A toy manufacturing factory has an annual capacity of 12,000 toys. If the fixed costs are rupees 1 lakh/year, variable cost rupees 20 per unit, and selling price rupees 40 per unit, the quantity to break-even is _____ units.

A. 5000
B. 300
C. 2500
D. None of these

Answer: A

Explanation:

$$\text{Break even point} = \frac{\text{Total fixed cost } (TFC)}{\text{Price per unit } (P) - \text{Variable cost } (V.C.)}$$

Given:

Total fixed cost (TFC) $= 100000, P = 40, VC = 20$.

$$\text{Break even point} = \frac{100000}{40-20} = 5000.$$

Hence, the quantity of break-even is 5000 units.

12. The fixed cost of the firm is Rs. 60,000/- per month. The variable cost is Rs. 10/- per unit and selling price is Rs. 50 per unit. The break even quantity will be:

A. 1300
B. 1400
C. 1500
D. 1600

Answer: C

Explanation:

$$\text{Break even quantity} = \frac{\text{Total fixed cost } (TFC)}{\text{Price per unit } (P) - \text{Variable cost } (V.C.)}$$

Calculation:
Given:
total fixed cost $= $ Rs 60,000 per month, variable cost $= $ Rs 10 per unit, price per unit $(P) = $ Rs 50 per unit

$$\text{Break even quantity} = \frac{\text{Total fixed cost } (TFC)}{\text{Price per unit } (P) - \text{Variable cost } (V.C.)}$$

$$\text{Break even quantity} = \frac{60000}{50-10} = \frac{60000}{40} = 1500$$

13. Breakeven point (BEP) indicates:

A. Recovery of fixed cost
B. Recovery of variable cost

| | **C.** Recovery of both of above costs | **D.** Recovery of fixed, variable costs and margin of profit |

Answer: C

Explanation:

Breakeven point (BEP) indicates Recovery of both of above costs.

14. An organization has decided to produce a new product. Fixed cost for producing the product is estimated as Rs. 1,00,000. Variable cost for producing the product is Rs. 100. Market survey indicated that the product selling price could be Rs. 200. The break-even quantity is:

| **A.** 1000 | **B.** 2000 |
| **C.** 500 | **D.** 900 |

Answer: A

Explanation:

Concept:

If x number of units are produced in the system then

Total sale $= sx$

Fixed cost $= F$

variable cost $= vx$

and Profit $= P_t$

where s is the sale cost per unit and v is the variable cost per unit

Total sale $=$ Total cost $+$ Profit

$sx = F + vx + P$

At break-even point, Profit $(P) = 0$

So, $sx = F + vx$

$$x = \frac{F}{s - v}$$

Calculation:

Given, $F = 100000$ Rs., $v = 100$ Rs. and $s = 200$ Rs.

Then,

$$x = \frac{100000}{200 - 100} = 1000 \text{ units}$$

15. The risk of return from investment can be measured through:

| **A.** Variability of rates of return from average rate of return as derived in the form of standard deviation | **B.** Variability of rates of return from average rate of return as derived in the form of median |
| **C.** Comparison of return from investment with industry returns | **D.** Comparison of return from investment with competitor's return |

Answer: A

Explanation:

The risk of return from investment can be measured through Variability of rates of return from average rate of return as derived in the form of standard deviation.

16. Which methods of risk analysis better serve lender's perspective in the capital budgeting decisions?

| **A.** Certainty Equivalent approach | **B.** Decision Analysis |
| **C.** Risk Adjusted Discount Rate | **D.** Simulation and Sensitivity analyses |

Answer: A

Explanation:

The certainty equivalent approach involves adjusting the expected cash flows of a project to account for the level of risk involved.

17. Political risk management comes in the ambit of which of the following financial decisions?

| **A.** Non - conventional capital budgeting | **B.** International currency arbitrage |
| **C.** Foreign exchange market | **D.** Multinational capital budgeting |

Answer: D

Explanation:

Political risk management comes in the ambit of Multinational capital budgeting financial decisions.

18. Which one of the following analyses is suitable for risk-return analysis in financial decisions?

| **A.** CAPM analysis | **B.** SWOT analysis |

C. Capital gearing   **D.** EVA analysis

Answer: A

Explanation:

The Capital Asset Pricing Model (CAPM) describes the relationship between systematic risk and expected return for assets, particularly stocks.

19. Which of the following securities has the most possible risk as well as the highest potential return?

    A. Preferred stocks   **B.** Commercial paper

    C. Derivative securities   **D.** Bonds

Answer: A

Explanation:

Derivatives are contracts that allow corporations, investors, and municipalities to transfer the risks and rewards of commercial or financial events to third parties. Holding a derivative contract reduces the risk of poor harvests, market volatility, or unfavourable occurrences such as a bond default.

20. _________ type of risk can be avoided by diversifying properly.

    A. Systematic risk   **B.** Unsystematic risk

    C. Portfolio risk   **D.** Total risk

Answer: B

Explanation:

Diversification can help to mitigate unsystematic risk, which is also known as diversifiable risk. Investors are still exposed to market-wide systemic risk even after diversification. The unsystematic risk with systematic risk equals total risk.

Introduction

Resource mobilization is when a business or organization secures new or additional resources to meet needs. This process can also include strategies that maximize the efficiency of existing resources. In some cases, organizations may take count of what's currently available and develop a plan to use those resources as efficiently as possible. If necessary, the business can acquire new or enhanced resources to supplement any existing options. Especially in times of great business need or demand, it can be important to understand what an organization has and needs to successfully cover expenses and maintain standard quality.

Resource mobilisation refers to the coordination of all activities involved in securing new and additional resources for an organisation. It involves mobilisation of resources from outside the enterprise. Taking affective measures to make the best utilisation of existing resources is also considered as mobilisation of resources. It is often termed as new business development. Mobilisation can be explained through the five Ms. They are:

Resource mobilization is important to an organization for these reasons

Allows the company to continue service for customers: By making sure that a business always has the required resources to meet customer demand, it can guarantee that customers never experience dips in service. This can create loyal and long-lasting customer relationships with the company, which can make strong relationships with customers that can be influential to its success. Maintains sustainability: If a business is to sustain its operations, then it may require sufficient resources to successfully complete regular tasks and projects. Understanding the number of resources necessary to sustain business practices can help maintain regular production in the event of great demand or any challenges.

Leads to product and service improvement: If an organization isn't struggling to find sufficient resources and has complied extra resources for the case of emergency, then it can focus its energy on improving products or services rather than worrying about resource acquisition. In a regular resource mobilization cycle, a business can spend designed time periods acquiring resources, and it can follow this period with innovation and advancement.

Helps a business expand: To expand its operations, a business can consider generating new products and services and acquiring new customers. To do this, the business may need the correct amount of available resources.

Types of Resources

Here are the four types of resources in business:

1. Physical resources

Physical resources are tangible assets that a company may use to create and distribute its products or services. Some examples of physical resources include equipment, production or storage facilities and inventory. Even if a company doesn't offer a tangible product, it can still use physical resources. For example, you can consider distribution elements like transport vehicles or promotional items like brochures to be physical resources.

2. Human resources

Human resources are employees who help a business run. This can include those who help develop the concepts, ideas and strategies for the business and its products. It can also include the employees who create, transport or sell the product or service. Like other resource types, human resources can be a crucial aspect of an organization. Mobilizing employees as resources can involve hiring new staff or developing training opportunities to improve the performance and output of current employees.

3. Intellectual resources

Intellectual resources can include any nontangible resources that allow a business to operate successfully. Some examples of intellectual resources include product patents, any branding content, copyright materials or partnerships with other institutions. Data can also be an intellectual resource. Information about important topics like customer satisfaction or purchasing habits can greatly influence the business' performance and decision-making. In some cases, intellectual resources can include the knowledge and expertise of employees. In this way, intellectual resources can overlap with human resources.

4. Financial resources

Financial resources are the monetary sources an organization can use to complete goals. Some types of financial resources include cash, credit, lines of credit or stocks. In many cases, financial resources are an important aspect of securing other resource types.

For example, you can use a company's available financial resources to purchase the physical resources, like packaging and manufacturing machinery, that can go into creating a new product.

What is sustainability in resource mobilization?
Sustainability in resource mobilization refers to the goal that an organization may have to obtain sufficient resources for continued business practice. Here are the three types of sustainability you may consider when mobilizing resources:

1. Programmatic sustainability
Programmatic sustainability is an organization's ability to consistently create and deliver quality products and services to customers. If it can sustain the ability to understand customer needs and create products to match those needs, then a business can enjoy high programmatic sustainability. This also involves the ability for a business to consistently expand its client base into new markets and locations.

2. Institutional sustainability
Institutional sustainability refers to a company's internal strength and ability to stay successful as an organization through structure and policy. This type of sustainability comes when an organization can develop strong but flexible structures and effective governing practices. Creating an institutionally sustainable organization requires well-supported and constantly evolving strategies that improve the experience of customers and employees. It also requires strong leadership to develop and improve policies.

3. Financial sustainability
Financial stability is an organization's ability to consistently maintain the proper financial resources to grow and improve. In many cases, financially stable businesses have various revenue sources from which to draw. These businesses might also have solid investments and stock options. Since businesses may run into unexpected problems or challenges, financial stability often requires sufficient and diversified financial resource streams to support business operation if revenue suddenly decreases.

Capital Market: Concept

Capital market is a place where buyers and sellers indulge in trade (buying/selling) of financial securities like bonds, stocks, etc. The trading is undertaken by participants such as individuals and institutions.

Capital market trades mostly in long-term securities. The magnitude of a nation's capital markets is directly interconnected to the size of its economy which means that ripples in one corner can cause major waves somewhere else.

Types of Capital Market
Capital market consists of two types i.e. Primary and Secondary.

Primary Market
Primary market is the market for new shares or securities. A primary market is one in which a company issues new securities in exchange for cash from an investor (buyer).It deals with trade of new issues of stocks and other securities sold to the investors.

Secondary Market
Secondary market deals with the exchange of prevailing or previously-issued securities among investors. Once new securities have been sold in the primary market, an efficient manner must exist for their resale. Secondary markets give investors the means to resell/ trade existing securities.Another important division in the capital market is made on the basis of the nature of security sold or bought, i.e. stock market and bond market.

Primary Market: Concept, Methods of issue

A primary market is a source of new securities. Often on an exchange, it's where companies, governments, and other groups go to obtain financing through debt-based or equity-based securities. Primary markets are facilitated by underwriting groups consisting of investment banks that set a beginning price range for a given security and oversee its sale to investors.

Companies and government entities sell new issues of common and preferred stock, corporate bonds and government bonds, notes, and bills on the primary market to fund business improvements or expand operations. Although an investment bank may set the securities' initial price and receive a fee for facilitating sales, most of the money raised from the sales goes to the issuer.

Functions of Primary Market
The functions of such a market are manifold:

New Issue Offer: The primary market organises offer of a new issue which had not been traded on any other exchange earlier. Due to this reason, it is also called a New Issue Market.

Organising new issue offers involves a detailed assessment of project viability, among other factors. The financial arrangements for the purpose include considerations of promoters' equity, liquidity ratio, debt-equity ratio and requirement of foreign exchange.

Underwriting Services: Underwriting is an essential aspect while offering a new issue. An underwriter's role in a primary marketplace includes purchasing unsold shares if it cannot manage to sell the required number of shares to the public. A financial institution may act as an underwriter, earning a commission on underwriting.

Investors rely on underwriters for determining whether undertaking the risk would be worth its returns. It may so happen that an underwriter ends up buying all the IPO issue, and subsequently selling it to investors.

Distribution of New Issue: A new issue is also distributed in a primary marketing sphere. Such distribution is initiated with a new prospectus issue. It invites the public at large to buy a new issue and provides detailed information on the company, issue, and involved underwriters.

Types of Primary Market Issues

An initial public offering, or IPO, is an example of a security issued on a primary market. An IPO occurs when a private company sells shares of stock to the public for the first time, a process known as "going public." The process, including the original price of the new shares, is set by a designated investment bank, hired by the company to do the initial underwriting for a particular stock.

For example, company ABCWXYZ Inc. hires five underwriting firms to determine the financial details of its IPO. The underwriters detail that the issue price of the stock will be $15. Investors can then buy the IPO at this price directly from the issuing company. This is the first opportunity that investors have to contribute capital to a company through the purchase of its stock. A company's equity capital is comprised of the funds generated by the sale of stock on the primary market.

A rights offering (issue) permits companies to raise additional equity through the primary market after already having securities enter the secondary market. Current investors are offered prorated rights based on the shares they currently own, and others can invest anew in newly minted shares.

Private Placement and Primary Market

Other types of primary market offerings for stocks include private placement and preferential allotment. Private placement allows companies to sell directly to more significant investors such as hedge funds and banks without making shares publicly available. Preferential allotment offers shares to select investors (usually hedge funds, banks, and mutual funds) at a special price not available to the general public.

Similarly, businesses and governments that want to generate debt capital can choose to issue new short- and long-term bonds on the primary market. New bonds are issued with coupon rates that correspond to the current interest rates at the time of issuance, which may be higher or lower than those offered by pre-existing bonds.

Angel Investor

An angel investor (also known as a private investor, seed investor or angel funder) is a high-net-worth individual who provides financial backing for small startups or entrepreneurs, typically in exchange for ownership equity in the company. Often, angel investors are found among an entrepreneur's family and friends. The funds that angel investors provide may be a one-time investment to help the business get off the ground or an ongoing injection to support and carry the company through its difficult early stages.

Origins of Angel Investors

The term "angel" came from the Broadway theater, when wealthy individuals gave money to propel theatrical productions. The term "angel investor" was first used by the University of New Hampshire's William Wetzel, founder of the Center for Venture Research. Wetzel completed a study on how entrepreneurs gathered capital.

An angel investor is a high-net-worth individual who provides financial backing for small startups or entrepreneurs, typically in exchange for ownership equity in the company. Often, angel investors are found among an entrepreneur's family and friends. The funds that angel investors provide may be a one-time investment to help the business get off the ground or an ongoing injection to support and carry the company through its difficult early stages.

Angel investors usually give support to start-ups at the initial moments (where risks of the start-ups failing are relatively high) and when most investors are not prepared to back them. A small but increasing number of angel investors invest online through equity crowdfunding or organize themselves into angel groups or angel networks to share investment capital, as well as to provide advice to their portfolio companies. Over the last 50 years, the number of angel investors has greatly increased.

Features

- An angel investor is usually a high-net-worth individual who funds startups at the early stages, often with their own money.
- Angel investing is often the primary source of funding for many startups who find it more appealing than other, more predatory, forms of funding.
- The support that angel investors provide startups fosters innovation which translates into economic growth.
- These types of investments are risky and usually do not represent more than 10% of the angel investor's portfolio.

Importance of Angel Financing

- They are more focused on the commitment and passion of the founders and the larger market opportunities that they have identified.
- An Angel investor plays a vital role in the development of the economy by providing the risk capital which contributes to the economic growth and technological advances.
- Early financing of the start-ups to some extent has become more dependent on angel investors, as they provide loans on relatively easier interest rates, unlike venture capital. The venture capital funds demand aggressive revenue growth quickly and are not able to accommodate a large number of small deals. The traditional source of start-up and early-stage financing-bank lending is limited due to its risk level and handling costs.
- Further, professional angel investors look for defined exit strategy or acquisitions or initial public offerings (IPOs). Due to the least interest in giving their money back or generate any return
- Angel investors make a prominent difference with a startup's success as well as its failure. Most of the times, they are the first and foremost investors.
- The effective internal rate of return for a successful portfolio investor ranges from 20% to 30%. This is beneficial for the investors and for entrepreneurs, who are the primary sources of financing. Hence makes angel investment perfect for entrepreneurs who are financially struggling during the initial phase of their business.

Venture Capital

Venture capital is a tool for funding businesses and an avenue for wealthy individuals and large investors to engage, contribute and invest. Wealthy investors favor making long-term growth investments in companies with their capital. This funding is known as venture capital, and the investors are known as venture capitalists; in other terms, it is a way for businesses to get money fast and for investors to build their assets over time.

Venture capitalists frequently invest in startups, and while these kinds of investments are hazardous due to their lack of liquidity, they also have the potential to produce spectacular returns in the right circumstances. This article discusses everything from what is venture capital and venture capital meaning to its types, features, and much more. Let's take a close look at its meaning first.

What is the Process of Venture Capital?

Venture capitalists typically work for venture capital businesses that raise money from external investors, unlike angel investors who invest their own money. High net-worth individuals, large corporates, and investment firms like pension funds and insurance companies might be included in this group of investors, referred to as limited partners.

Venture capitalists spend the money they raise on companies with the potential for rapid growth or have already experienced impressive growth. The many stages of venture capital financing correspond to the various stages of a company's development. Startups frequently go through these phases as they develop and obtain funding from venture capital firms on various occasions.

While some Venture capital firms specialize in a particular stage, others take a more general approach and invest in businesses at many stages of the company's lifecycle. For instance, seed-stage investors support the development of early-stage startups, whereas late-stage investors support the expansion of established businesses. Numerous VC firms focus their investments on a specific business or industry vertical.

Businesses can frequently access substantial amounts of funding through Venture capital. They can actively contribute to the company's success by making strategic (occasionally operational) choices. Additionally, the proper investor brings value to the business by contributing their knowledge, expertise, and contacts. An investor frequently requests to join the company's board of directors as an official managing partner or board member as part of a venture capital arrangement.

Features of Venture Capital

The characteristics of venture capital are as follows:

- It mainly focuses on financing young businesses that are having trouble entering the capital market in their initial stages of growth.
- To provide a fixed return for the venture capital sources, this financing may also be loan-based or in the form of inconvertible debt securities.
- Investors in venture capital seek to profit financially from the success of the business that borrows.
- It is an investment for the long term and is placed in businesses with strong growth prospects. The allocation of venture capital will result in the company's quick expansion.
- The venture capital provider will also participate in the borrowing business; in doing so, they will provide financial support and managerial expertise.

Advantages of Venture Capital

- Venture capitalists present a chance for growth
- Venture capitalists facilitate networking.
- Businesses can raise a significant amount of money.
- Guidance, advice, and knowledge can be found in venture capital.
- No commitment to pay back the capital investment
- Generally speaking, venture capitalists are reliable.
- Venture capitalists can aid in team building and hiring.

Disadvantages Of Venture Capital

- It can be challenging to approach a venture capitalist.
- A decision from a venture capitalist is typically made slowly.
- The search for investors may divert an entrepreneur's focus.
- The founder's ownership interest is diminished.
- It is necessary to exercise extensive due diligence.
- Rapid growth for the business is anticipated.
- A performance schedule is used to release funds.

Funding

Funding is the act of providing resources to finance a need, program, or project. While this is usually in the form of money, it can also take the form of effort or time from an organization or company. Generally, this word is used when a firm uses its internal reserves to satisfy its necessity for cash, while the term financing is used when the firm acquires capital from external sources. [citation needed]

Sources of funding include credit, venture capital, donations, grants, savings, subsidies, and taxes. Fundings such as donations, subsidies, and grants that have no direct requirement for return of investment are described as "soft funding" or "crowdfunding". Funding that facilitates the exchange of equity ownership in a company for capital investment via an online funding portal per the Jumpstart Our Business Startups Act (alternately, the "JOBS Act of 2012") (U.S.) is known as equity crowdfunding.

Multiple Choice Questions

1. Which of these is NOT a part of capital receipt?
   - **A.** Recovery of loan
   - **B.** Disinvestment
   - **C.** Borrowing
   - **D.** Tax

Answer: D

Explanation:

Tax is considered as the part of revenue receipt and many more such as profits, interest earned incomes from other sources, etc.

2. Capital markets denote the places where funds are swapped between:
   - **A.** suppliers of capital
   - **B.** Borrower of capital
   - **C.** Those who request capital investments.
   - **D.** Both (a) & (c)

Answer: D

Explanation:

Capital markets are also considered as the financial markets which bring sellers and buyers with each other to trade stocks, currencies, bonds, and other economic possessions. Capital markets generally comprise the bond market and the stock market.

3. Primary capital markets are the platform where:
   - **A.** New securities are issued
   - **B.** New securities are sold
   - **C.** New securities are borrowed
   - **D.** Both (a) Both (a) and (b)

Answer: D

Explanation:

Primary capital markets are the platform where new securities are issued and new securities are sold.

4. The secondary market is a platform in which:
    A. Only earlier allotted securities are being traded among investors.
    B. Investors trade in new securities
    C. Individually cannot participate
    D. None of these

Answer: A

Explanation:

The secondary market is a platform in which only earlier allotted securities are being traded among investors.

5. What are the best-known capital markets?
    A. The stock market
    B. The bond markets
    C. A depository account with any of the depositories in India
    D. Both (a) & (b)

Answer: D

Explanation:

Due to the vital functioning of the bond market and stock market, they are also known as the primary and secondary capital markets.

6. Businesses in capital markets are normally managed by:
    A. Governmental treasury departments and sometimes accessed by the public, also
    B. Private bodies in the financial sectors
    C. International bodies and businesses
    D. None of the above

Answer: A

Explanation:

The capital market is the governmental organization that deals in the connection of buyers and suppliers and also provides financial support to the required businesses.

7. What is Net Present Value?
    A. Net present value is, which displays the cash flow.
    B. Value for both outflow and inflow.
    C. Net Present Value is the sum of the available values of cash flow
    D. None of the above

Answer: C

Explanation:

NVP (Net present value) is defined as the alteration between the present value of cash outflows and the present value of cash inflows during a period of time.

8. Which is the standardized process for the analysis of capital budgeting and also known as future cash flow subtracted from the purchase price?
    A. SEBI
    B. Net Present Value NPV
    C. RBI Reserve Bank of India
    D. IRDA

Answer: C

Explanation:

The RBI (Reserve Bank of India) is India's only central bank and governing body accountable for guidelines of the banking systems of India. RBI is under the regulations and ownership of the Finance Ministry of the government of India.

9. What "rights issue" do the shareholders of a company have under the Companies Act, 1956?
    A. Voting rights of the shareholder members of each affiliate of a public company that contains the shares equity and possesses votes in proportions.
    B. First Board Meeting: The board meeting was held, and the resolution for issuing the right shares was passed, and the right issue does not need the approval of shareholders.
    C. Issue a letter of the offer without the approval of shareholders
    D. None of the above

Answer: A

Explanation:

Voting rights of the shareholder members of each affiliate of a public company that contains the shares equity and possesses votes in proportions "rights issue" do the shareholders of a company have under the Companies Act, 1956.

10. What are the eligibility criteria for a listed company to make a public issue?

A.	Company should have predictable and consistent revenue, and the company should have enough money to pay for the process of IPO. Moreover, companies should be key players in the industry.	**B.**	The company should contain a minimum of Rs 3 crore in net tangible possessions in the recent three years
C.	The company's continuous growth is not required.	**D.**	Both (a) & (b)

Answer: D

Explanation:

The company should have predictable and consistent revenue, and the company should have enough money to pay for the process of IPO. Moreover, companies should be key players in the industry, The company should contain a minimum of Rs 3 crore in net tangible possessions in the recent three years are the eligibility criteria for a listed company to make a public issue.

11. Which of the subsequent establishments delivers a guarantee or assurance to the exporters?

A.	Exim Bank	**B.**	Director General Foreign Trade
C.	Reserve Bank of India	**D.**	Export Credit Guarantee Corporation (E C G C)

Answer: D

Explanation:

Maintained by the Government of India and was established in 1957 with the aim of promoting exports from the nation by managing and providing export-related services and credit risk insurance.

12. Which of the succeeding administrations issues the guidelines for global trade?

A.	World Bank	**B.**	World Trade Organization
C.	Foreign Exchange Dealers' Association	**D.**	Directorate General of Foreign Trade

Answer: B

Explanation:

WTO is the only global worldwide organization working with the guidelines and rules of businesses and trades between the nations.

13. What is a cross-border exchange?

A.	Trading of foreign currency in India.	**B.**	The trading of the Indian rupee in exchange for other currencies/ goods.
C.	Hawala transactions in Indian rupee.	**D.**	Unauthorised remittance of the Indian rupee.

Answer: B

Explanation:

The cross-border exchange may be defined as the exchange of goods and services between the two countries is known as the cross-border exchange.

14. The capital market is organized in India by:

A.	RBI	**B.**	NABARD
C.	SEBI	**D.**	IRDA

Answer: C

Explanation:

SEBI is known as an important part of the Indian financial system as it regulates and monitors the stock market and defends the benefits of the investors by imposing certain rules and protocols.

15. Which of the below-mentioned is not the objective of SEBI?

A.	To regulate the securities market	**B.**	To protect the interests of inventors
C.	To promote individual businesses	**D.**	To promote the development of the market

Answer: C

Explanation:

SEBI may be defined as a government organization that works on assisting in providing investments to the investors in a totally transparent environment of investment.

www.ingramcontent.com/pod-product-compliance
Lightning Source LLC
La Vergne TN
LVHW080549200726
843510LV00008B/1059